# PRAISE FOR
# CARLTON

"Easily the craziest, weirdest, strangest, funniest, most obscene writer in America."
—*GOTHIC MAGAZINE*

"Carlton Mellick III has the craziest book titles... and the kinkiest fans!"
—CHRISTOPHER MOORE, author of *The Stupidest Angel*

"If you haven't read Mellick you're not nearly perverse enough for the twenty first century."
—JACK KETCHUM, author of *The Girl Next Door*

"Carlton Mellick III is one of bizarro fiction's most talented practitioners, a virtuoso of the surreal, science fictional tale."
—CORY DOCTOROW, author of *Little Brother*

"Bizarre, twisted, and emotionally raw—Carlton Mellick's fiction is the literary equivalent of putting your brain in a blender."
—BRIAN KEENE, author of *The Rising*

"Carlton Mellick III exemplifies the intelligence and wit that lurks between its lurid covers. In a genre where crude titles are an art in themselves, Mellick is a true artist."
—*THE GUARDIAN*

"Just as Pop had Andy Warhol and Dada Tristan Tzara, the bizarro movement has its very own P. T. Barnum-type practitioner. He's the mutton-chopped author of such books as *Electric Jesus Corpse* and *The Menstruating Mall*, the illustrator, editor, and instructor of all things bizarro, and his name is Carlton Mellick III."
—*DETAILS MAGAZINE*

"The most original novelist working today? The most outrageous? The most unpredictable? These aren't easy superlatives to make; however, Carlton Mellick may well be all of those things, behind a canon of books that all irreverently depart from the form and concepts of traditional novels, and adventure the reader into a howling, dark fantasyland of the most bizarre, over-the-top, and mind-warping inventiveness."
—EDWARD LEE, author of *Header*

"Discussing Bizarro literature without mentioning Mellick is like discussing weird-ass muttonchopped authors without mentioning Mellick."
—*CRACKED.COM*

"Carlton is an acquired taste, but he hooks you like a drug."
—HUNTER SHEA, author of *Forest of Shadows*

"Mellick's career is impressive because, despite the fact that he puts out a few books a year, he has managed to bring something new to the table every time… Every Mellick novel is packed with more wildly original concepts than you could find in the current top ten *New York Times* bestsellers put together."
—*VERBICIDE*

"Mellick's guerrilla incursions combine total geekboy fandom and love with genuine, unbridled outsider madness. As such, it borders on genius, in the way only true outsider art can."
—*FANGORIA*

# Also by
# Carlton Mellick III

**Satan Burger**
**Electric Jesus Corpse** (Fan Club Exclusive)
**Sunset With a Beard** (stories)
**Razor Wire Pubic Hair**
**Teeth and Tongue Landscape**
**The Steel Breakfast Era**
**The Baby Jesus Butt Plug**
**Fishy-fleshed**
**The Menstruating Mall**
**Ocean of Lard** (with Kevin L. Donihe)
**Punk Land**
**Sex and Death in Television Town**
**Sea of the Patchwork Cats**
**The Haunted Vagina**
**Cancer-cute** (Fan Club Exclusive)
**War Slut**
**Sausagey Santa**
**Ugly Heaven**
**Adolf in Wonderland**
**Ultra Fuckers**
**Cybernetrix**
**The Egg Man**
**Apeshit**
**The Faggiest Vampire**
**The Cannibals of Candyland**
**Warrior Wolf Women of the Wasteland**
**The Kobold Wizard's Dildo of Enlightenment +2**
**Zombies and Shit**

**Crab Town**
**The Morbidly Obese Ninja**
**Barbarian Beast Bitches of the Badlands**
**Fantastic Orgy** (stories)
**I Knocked Up Satan's Daughter**
**Armadillo Fists**
**The Handsome Squirm**
**Tumor Fruit**
**Kill Ball**
**Cuddly Holocaust**
**Hammer Wives** (stories)
**Village of the Mermaids**
**Quicksand House**
**Clusterfuck**
**Hungry Bug**
**Tick People**
**Sweet Story**
**As She Stabbed Me Gently in the Face**
**ClownFellas: Tales of the Bozo Family**
**Bio Melt**
**Every Time We Meet at the Dairy Queen, Your Whole Fucking Face Explodes**
**The Terrible Thing That Happens**

# EXERCISE BIKE

## CARLTON MELLICK III
ERASERHEAD PRESS
PORTLAND, OREGON

ERASERHEAD PRESS
P.O. BOX 10065
PORTLAND, OR 97296

WWW.ERASERHEADPRESS.COM

ISBN: 978-1-62105-222-7

Copyright © 2016 by Carlton Mellick III

Cover art copyright © 2016 by Ed Mironiuk
www.edmironiuk.com

All rights reserved. No part of this book may be reproduced or transmitted in any form or by any means, electronic or mechanical, including photocopying, recording, or by any information storage and retrieval system, without the written consent of the publisher, except where permitted by law.

Printed in the USA.

# AUTHOR'S NOTE

So one of the biggest problems with being a fulltime writer is that it's very difficult to stay in good shape unless you work really hard at it. Spending most of your time at home, sitting in a cozy chair, typing out stories behind a desk, barely ever leaving the house, there's not a whole lot of exercise you're going to get. I write most of my books marathon-style, where I do nothing but write for fifteen hours a day until a book is done. I don't get any exercise. I mostly eat crap food like microwave cheeseburgers and frozen pizzas. By the time I finish a book I feel like absolute death.

The only way I'm able to get any exercise at all is if I go on a health marathon, which is similar to a writing marathon but instead of writing I spend fifteen hours a day doing pushups, riding an exercise bike, and sometimes fasting. I go on health marathons for a couple months a year, usually once I feel too shitty to get anything else done, typically in September or October.

I came up with the idea for this book while I was on one of these health marathons a couple of years ago. I was riding my exercise bike, watching k-pop videos, and came up with the idea to use *Exercise Bike* as the title of a story. For some reason, the title appealed to me. Maybe because it's not a typical title I'd use for a book. Then, while pedaling and sweating, I imagined what it would be like to ride a human exercise bike. The story quickly formed in my head after that.

Exercise Bike was originally going to be a short story, but I had too many ideas I wanted to play with to make it too short. I was especially interested in setting the story in a dystopian world where junk food was outlawed and calories severely limited. The funny thing is that I kind of like the idea of living in a world like this. Sure it would suck all the enjoyment out of eating, but it would make things a lot easier for somebody like me to stay in shape. Fun fact: The apartment of this story is based around my current home. I live in a three story condo where the living room and kitchen are upstairs, the bedrooms are downstairs, and the garage is on the bottom floor. There aren't any wasp nests in my walls, however, but when I was a kid I lived in a house where the walls were infested with bees. Bees used to fly around my bedroom like ordinary houseflies, landing on my arms and in my hair. I used to have to brush them out of my bed before going to sleep every night.

I've never been stung by a bee, so I'm not sure if I'm allergic or not. It was just so normal to me back then that I never really minded them all that much. But thinking back on the experience, I realized it was kind of an interesting thing to have walls filled with beehives, so I wanted to put it in a story. I chose to use wasps instead of bees though, because wasps are far more freaky to me than bees. In fact, wasps are probably the freakiest insects of them all. Some people are freaked out by spiders, but wasps are like spiders with fucking wings. And the bastards sting the fuck out of everything they come across just because they feel like it.

Fuck wasps.

—Carlton Mellick III  4/12/2016 4:15pm

# CHAPTER ONE

Tori is addicted to eating wasps. She eats them alive, first licking their wings until they are too wet to fly away. Then, one at a time, she puts them in her mouth and sucks on their smooth abdomens until they sting her tongue. The sensation is intense. Intoxicating. Like eating the spiciest of chili peppers. After three stings, she chews up the insect, swallows, and moves onto the next wasp.

Her mouth is always full of sores. Swollen burning lumps on her lips, inner cheeks, uvula, and that delicate squishy flesh beneath her tongue. But this doesn't stop her from eating them by the dozen.

It wasn't an addiction she was born with. Not some hidden fetish she discovered in herself later in life. No, it was something she grew to crave. But it started as a necessity. A way to satisfy her hunger. You see, Tori has an unusually fast metabolism and requires far more than her allotted calories per day. She has to get her extra calories from somewhere, even if she has to resort to eating bugs.

She'd prefer not to eat bugs. In fact, she'd love to get by with eating only 2000 calories per day like everyone else. But she has a hard time keeping her hunger under control. It's very common for her to fly through her calories without even realizing it.

"I'll take a Black Bean Big Mac and an eight piece Tofu McNuggets," Tori says, placing an order at McDonald's during her lunch break. "I'll also have a Soyrizo Sandwich, an extra large McCarrot Fries, and a medium Dr. Kombucha."

The teenager behind the cash register looks at her in shock for ordering so much, but Tori is used to the expression. It's the same response she gets every time she orders food in public. He just looks at her for a moment, then looks back at the register. He thinks she's fucking with him.

In a shaky voice, he says, "Okay… that'll be eighteen fifty-seven and one thousand three hundred and twenty-six calories."

Tori hands him her debit card and calorie card. He runs the calorie card first.

"I'm sorry, Miss, but you only have one hundred and sixty-five calories left on your card."

"What?" Tori cries, leaning over the counter to look at the screen on the register. "That's impossible."

"That's what it says. I'm sorry, but you won't be able to order that much."

Tori can't believe she's down to 165. It's only lunch time. She had no idea she spent so many calories on breakfast and snacks.

"Well, what can I get for 165?"

He sighs and shakes his head, trying to do math. "Just a small McCarrot Fries and a couple ketchups. I guess."

Tori clenches her fist and shivers with hunger. She fights the urge to jump over the counter and eat the cashier's greasy pimpled flesh right off of his face, then ask him how many calories that would be.

It takes all of her willpower to calm herself. "Fine. Just give me that."

Tori sits down at a table near the garbage can, eating her hot carrot sticks in less than a minute. She doesn't leave right after she's finished. She lingers by the trash can, waiting for somebody to throw away a half-eaten burger or a soggy tofu nugget. It's a technique she's used several times in the past to get extra calories. She'll see someone coming toward the trash with unfinished food on their tray, then she'll offer to throw it away for them. It's illegal to eat other people's calories or steal food from the trash, but when she's hungry enough she finds it's worth the risk.

"Fucking McDonald's," a man says, slamming his food tray on the counter next to Tori. He's a tall, large-boned man that Tori has seen eating here at lunch from time to time. He looks at her as he gathers napkins and a plastic fork. "Do you believe this shit? They fucked up my order and gave me a Southwest Salad instead of a Black Bean Big Mac. The salad is the most fattening thing on the menu. Three times the calories as the Big Mac. It's bullshit."

"They wouldn't change the order?" Tori asks.

He shakes his head and sits down at the table next to her. "No, they can't reverse the calorie charge. They gave it to me for free, but I don't care about the money. I want the calories back. I probably can't eat dinner now."

"Join the club," Tori says. "I haven't eaten dinner since Thursday."

The man looks Tori up and down. She's all skin and bones. Not an ounce of fat on her body. Based on her appearance, she doesn't seem like the kind of person who blows through calories so easily.

"Dave," he says, holding out his hand to introduce himself.

She shakes his hand. "Tori."

It's not like her to engage with strange men in public, but having someone to talk to was getting her mind off of her stomach.

"I remember when McDonald's was actually good," Dave said, stirring the vegan chipotle ranch into his salad. "It was junk food. But that was the point. It was supposed to be bad for you. Do you remember what a Big Mac used to taste like?"

Tori nods. "Yeah. I never ate them much back then, but now that they're illegal I think I miss them more than anything. I never really liked fast food, but Big Macs were perfection. The way the secret sauce and lettuce mixed together. The perfect balance of cheese, meat and bread. I'd kill to have a *real* Big Mac again."

"They still have them in Japan. They're expensive as hell, but I might make the trip someday, just to have real junk food again."

Tori nods. She's fantasized about traveling to Japan for years. Because the Japanese didn't have the same problems with obesity that they had in the western world, they never implemented strict health laws like they did over here. You can go there and eat as many calories as you want without fear of being fined or put in jail. It's like Thanksgiving all year round.

"It's all bullshit," Dave says. He takes a bite of salad and shakes his head in disapproval. "Did you know the Black Bean Big Mac would actually have more calories than an original Big Mac if it wasn't a third the size? The black bean patty doesn't have as much fat as the old hamburger patty did, but it has a lot more calories. More carbs. I'd rather they just make mini Big Macs."

"They might have put them on the menu if beef wasn't outlawed."

"Beef…" Dave shakes his head. "That's a whole other pile of bullshit right there. We've been eating red meat for thousands of years. Taking that away from us is downright fascism."

"Of course it's fascism. They don't call them Health Nazis for nothing."

Dave smiles when Tori uses the term *Health Nazi*. It's like he's found a kindred spirit in her. Dave is obviously a small town conservative who despises the extreme leftists who are now running the government. But Tori doesn't see him as a kindred spirit. She's not a republican. She's a liberal all the way. It's just that she hates extremists. Left, right, it doesn't matter. She's against anyone who tries to push their moral agenda down other people's throats.

"You surprise me," Dave says. "You don't seem like the kind of person who would disapprove of the health laws."

"Why do you say that?"

"You're so skinny. You probably ate less than two thousand calories a day before it became mandatory."

Tori laughs out loud. Everyone in the McDonald's looks at her. "I used to eat twice that per meal. And I ate five meals a day."

Dave's expression explodes in surprise. "You're kidding me... Were you fat?"

"Not at all." Tori shakes her head. "I was always able to eat as much as I wanted without ever gaining weight. I have a really high metabolism. Like, *really* high."

"You're lucky."

"I *was* lucky," she says. "Now it's a curse. My body burns calories too fast. I'm never able to get enough to eat."

Dave sighs. "Damn. And I thought *I* had it rough. Being my size I was able to eat a lot as well, but nothing like that." He looks down into his salad. "It's just not right. Can't you get a doctor to issue you more calories?"

Tori shakes her head. "I tried, but no doctor will listen. They'll only issue extra calories for extreme cases and they don't think my condition is extreme enough. I've tried using illegal calorie cards under fake identities, but ended up getting caught. The ten thousand dollar fine and two hundred hours of community service wasn't worth it. I won't do that again."

"Ever thought about getting U-Fit exercise equipment?" Dave asks. "You can get extra calories that way."

"Isn't that just for rich people though? Last I heard their machines went for as much as a new car."

Dave shrugs. "They were pretty spendy when they

first came out, but I hear they're getting cheaper. You can also get them on a payment plan."

"I don't know," Tori says. "I never thought they'd be worth it. Don't you burn as many calories as you earn? Isn't that the point of those things?"

"Not necessarily." Dave pauses to smile. "I have a friend who got a U-Fit exercise bike and he didn't even exercise. He just spun the pedals without even sitting on it. The machine can't tell whether you're actually on the bike or not. You earn calories based on how many miles you put on it, so you can pedal it however you want."

"Really? I never thought of that."

Dave looks around the room to make sure no one is listening. Then he leans in and whispers, "Actually, I even know of a device you can buy that will do the pedaling for you. It's black market, but not exactly illegal. You can earn calories all day long without moving a muscle."

"Are you serious?"

"I hear you can get up to ten thousand extra calories a day with the really good ones."

"But wouldn't having all those extra calories on your card be suspicious?"

"Not for you. If a morbidly obese guy came into McDonald's with ten thousand extra calories he claimed to have earned through exercise it would be a different story. But nobody would suspect you of cheating. They'd assume you're just one of those exercise addicts."

"So where would I get one of these devices?" Tori asks.

Dave hushes her down, worried about who might be listening. "Here." He takes out a piece of paper and writes down a phone number. "Call me if you get an exercise bike. I'll see if I can't get you in touch with the guy I know."

"How much are they?"

"No idea. Probably not cheap."

Tori takes his phone number and then nods at him. "Thanks."

"No problem." He smiles, then pushes his salad toward her. "Hey, want my broccoli? I hate the stuff."

Tori doesn't think twice about it. "Sure."

She picks all the broccoli out of his salad with her skinny bare fingers, trying to be as quick and inconspicuous as possible. As she gobbles them down, Dave gives her a conspiratorial wink, like he's just found a new partner in crime.

After work, Tori heads to the U-Fit store at the uptown mall. Her hands shake with hunger. She hopes she can afford to get a bike. If she can get it home that day maybe she can even earn enough calories to eat dinner. It was hard getting through the day without much of a lunch. She typed at her computer with twitchy fingers, responding to all the emails her boss couldn't be bothered to respond to.

When she gets to the store, a skinny bald man with round tinted glasses stands in the center of the room, smiling at her as she enters.

# EXERCISE BIKE

"Welcome to U-Fit, are *you* ready to get *fit?*" he says, pumping his tiny fist in the air at her.

He probably uses that line fifty times a day, so his enthusiasm is forced and annoying. Tori isn't amused.

"I'm looking for an exercise bike," she says.

"Of course, of course, come this way."

The scrawny bald man brings her to the other side of the store, past the treadmills, elliptical machines, and stair-climbers.

"Are you sure I can't interest you in an elliptical machine?" he asks. "You can earn calories three times faster on an elliptical than a bike."

Tori shakes her head. "Is it cheaper than a bike?"

The salesman curls his right lip and looks at the ceiling, pretending to think about it. "There is one model that's price is comparable to some of the bikes."

Tori doesn't want to hear his sales pitch. "I just want your cheapest exercise bike."

He looks her up and down, trying to determine the value of her clothes. Target shoes, Forever 21 skirt, jewelry from The Bling Store—she's obviously not in the same income bracket as his usual clientele. He knows he won't be able to upsell her, so he resigns to showing her the cheapest piece of equipment in the store.

"This is our most modestly priced stationary bike," he says, leading her to a folding bike so small and fragile that it would surely break under the weight of anyone over one hundred and sixty pounds.

Tori examines it. She attempts to find a price tag but there's none to be seen. If she got one of these at

Walmart it would only be about fifty dollars. She knows it's going to be far more than that, however.

"How does it work?" she asks.

"Give me your calorie card," he says.

Tori digs in her purse and hands it to him. He inserts it into a small card reader on the side of the bike.

"Get on," he says. "Give it a shot."

Tori has to lift her skirt halfway to get onto the bike seat. She ignores the creepy salesman admiring her pale thighs as she puts her feet into the pedal slots.

"See," he points at the screen. "This shows you how many calories you earn. It also shows you distance travelled, pedals per second, and time ridden. All of these affect how many calories you can earn."

Tori nods. She pedals as fast as she can, trying to get as many calories on her card as possible. But after ten minutes, she's only earned thirty calories. It would take her hours to earn enough to eat dinner. The salesman doesn't allow her to pedal any more than that. He turns off the machine and helps her down.

"So what do you think?" he asks.

Tori nods. "I like it. How much?"

"This one is twenty-five."

"Twenty-five hundred?"

The salesman can't help but snicker. "Twenty-five thousand."

Tori couldn't believe it. She knew they were expensive but not that much. Not for the cheapest model.

"I hear you have payment plans," Tori says. "How does that work?"

"Yes, if you pass the credit check, the price can be divided into four monthly payments."

Tori's heart sinks in her chest. Even if she could afford over six thousand a month, she'd never pass the credit check.

She lowers her head. "I can't afford that."

He nods his head as though prepared for her response. "I'm sorry. U-Fit is hoping to one day produce more affordable models for low-income households, but until the technology advances the prices must remain firm."

Tori says, "I understand."

But she knows it's bullshit. The only reason the machines are expensive is because they know they can get away with it. Adding a card reader to a fifty dollar machine doesn't make it worth as much as a new BMW. The desperation for extra calories is what drives the price up. Kind of like how doctors can charge $150,000 to remove an appendix even though the operation only costs the hospital sixteen dollars. When people are desperate enough, they'll pay anything.

As Tori turns to walk out, the salesman stares at her ass. He examines her body up and down, licks the corner of his lip with a pink pointy tongue.

"Hold on," he says, before she leaves the store.

She turns back.

"There is one other possibility…" he says. But then something makes him hesitate. He shakes his head. "Nevermind…"

Tori steps toward him. "What?"

"I do have one other exercise bike, but I'm not sure

you're right for it."

"How much is it?"

"You can't buy this exercise bike. It's kind of… Let's just say it's a prototype. We're looking for somebody to test ride it."

"Test ride it? How much would I have to pay?"

The salesman shakes his head. "Not a cent. Actually, you would be paid for your services."

"You'd pay me?" Tori's eyes light up. "How much?"

"Two hundred thousand dollars," he says.

Tori nearly squeals at him. "Just for testing an exercise bike?"

"You'd have to sign a contract agreeing to use it for a full year," he says. "You can't return it or damage it during this period. You must take very good care of it or face severe penalties. Confidentiality is also very important."

She nods. "If that's all then sign me up. I'm in."

The salesman holds up his hands. "Not so fast. The bike has to check you out first. It gets to choose its test subject. And to be honest, it's been very picky. Over fifty candidates have been turned down already. I'm not sure if you're going to be the one."

Tori pauses and stares at him for a moment, confused by his words.

She says, "What do you mean it gets to choose? We're just talking about a bike, aren't we?"

Tori imagines some kind of high-tech machine with artificial intelligence.

"All will be explained to you if you meet its standards," he says, then he waves her toward him. "Come on. Let's see if you're a worthy candidate."

She steps cautiously toward him, wondering what the heck is going on with this mysterious piece of exercise equipment. He leads her to the back of the store and brings her into an "employees only" section. The petite bald man appears nervous. The whole situation is beginning to worry her.

"Stand here so it can see you," the salesman says, positioning her in front of a dark tinted window.

He pushes a buzzer, alerting whatever is on the other side of the glass. Then they wait. The salesman looks at Tori with her arms folded and pulls her limbs apart so that her breasts aren't hidden.

He says, "Pose like this."

The salesman does a sexy pose with his hip leaning into his hand.

"What?" she asks.

"Act like a model," he says, continuing his sexy pose.

She does as he says.

"Push your boobs out," he says.

He pushes his own chest forward to show her what he means.

"Are you fucking with me?"

"No, just do it." He grabs her shoulders and tries to lean her chest out.

She pushes away from him. "Touch me again and I'll break your fucking nose."

The salesman tries to turn her around, saying, "Show off your ass."

Tori doesn't know what comes over her. She thinks

this is some kind of sick game the salesman is playing. She feels like the butt of a joke. Whatever the reason, she slams her knuckles into his nose. Blood sprays across the glass on impact.

The wimpy salesman cries out when he sees the blood in his hands. He looks at Tori in shock. "What's your problem? I'm just doing my job…"

She wipes her bloody knuckles on her skirt and says, "I told you not to touch me."

The salesman grabs a sweatband from a nearby cart and holds it up to his nose to stop the bleeding. Tori is about to turn and leave when a green light flashes above the tinted window.

When the salesman sees it, he drops the sweatband from his nose and blood gushes down his chin.

"Oh my," he says. "It accepted. It actually accepted you."

"Really?" Tori looks up at the green light.

"I guess it likes tough bitches."

"Likes tough bitches?" she asks. "Why would a machine care?"

"Well, it's not exactly a machine."

"Then what is it?"

The salesman ignores her. He puts a key in the door and unlocks it.

"Come on," he says. "Let me introduce you to your new exercise bike."

# CHAPTER TWO

If Tori had known what was behind that door she never would have entered the room. But now it's too late. She sees it and the sight will be burned into her memory for the rest of her life.

"What the hell is that thing?" Tori asks.

"Meet The Darren II," says the salesman.

"What the fuck is The Darren II?"

Tori can't take her eyes off of the monstrous contraption. It's shaped like an exercise bike, but it's not exactly a machine. It's made of flesh. It's a living, breathing organism.

The salesman steps around the bike, admiring the fine craftsmanship. "The Darren II is unlike any other piece of equipment U-Fit has ever had the privilege of offering. It's the very first human exercise bike."

Tori shivers at the gurgling sounds it makes as the bike tries to breathe. It pulses and sweats as she steps closer. Tiny eyes stare at her from the back of the display screen.

"It's human?" Tori can't believe what she's seeing. She assumes she must be on a hidden camera show and at any minute a host is going to pop out and tell her it's all just an elaborate joke. "How is that possible?"

"It took millions of dollars and several years of reconstructive surgery to create the machine standing before you. It's a miracle of science."

Tori examines it more closely. She can tell this isn't a joke. It really is a human that has been turned into a bike. The handles were once arms, stripped of most of its flesh and held together with wires and support bars. She can see muscle and bone through a thick layer of skin. Blood pumps through veins from a tiny heart deep inside of the machine. Its pedals were once legs. Its ass and genitals form the bike seat. Its facial features have mostly been removed, apart from its eyes.

"So... it was once a person?" Tori asks.

The bike's gray eyes look up at her, admiring her figure. When they blink, she steps back.

"Yes," says the salesman. "His name was Darren Oscarson. I know it might be difficult for you to believe, but Darren was not turned into The Darren II against his will. It was all his idea. He was a very wealthy man whose deepest desire was to be transformed into a piece of exercise equipment, to be used by beautiful women such as yourself."

Tori can't believe anyone would ever want to do this to themselves. Why would a man ever want to be permanently turned into a machine? Even if it was because of a sexual fetish, it's still far too extreme. The man must've been completely insane.

"Come on," the salesman says, patting the bike's fleshy seat. "Give it a try."

Tori looks at the bike. The bike looks back at her. The penis dangling from the front of the seat grows erect with anticipation.

"No fucking way," she says.

Then she gets the fuck out of there.

The salesman chases after her.

Before she gets out of the store, he says, "Two hundred thousand."

She pauses in the doorway.

"Are you sure you want to turn that down?" he asks.

She can't decide. She could really use that money. She could even quit her job for a year. But would the money really be worth having to ride that atrocity?

The salesman steps closer, "You'll also earn extra calories. The Darren II is much more liberal with dispensing calories than other bikes. You'll earn three times as much as you would with a normal bike."

Tori still can't move. She can't agree to ride the thing, but she can't refuse the offer either.

"If you walk out that door you might not get another chance," says the salesman. "Do you know how many women *wish* they were good enough for The Darren II? Do you know just how great of an opportunity you've been given? Hell, if the bike was into men I would have agreed to ride it in a heartbeat."

Tori can't believe what she's doing. All respect she's

ever had for herself melts away as she closes the door and returns to the salesman.

She says, "Fine. Tell me what I have to do."

A wide creepy smile returns to the salesman's face.

Tori goes over pages and pages of paperwork, signing and initialing every paragraph.

"Even though The Darren II was once human, you are to treat him as a normal piece of exercise equipment," says the salesman, handing her more and more paperwork to fill out. "You shouldn't talk to it, play music for it, or give it special treatment of any kind. In fact, it would be best if you just treat it as an ordinary exercise bike."

Tori just sighs with aggravation, shaking her head. She has no idea how it will be possible to pretend it's anything but a bike-shaped man she will be riding.

The salesman points at a paragraph detailing how to care for the bike. "The only thing you'll have to worry about is feeding it and cleaning it. You also must keep it inside. Don't store it in a garage or patio. Your house temperature must be at least eighty degrees. If it has any problems you should call this number." He points at an emergency contact number.

"What kind of problems?" Tori asks.

"The Darren II hasn't been extensively tested," says the salesman. "Keep an eye out for swelling or bruising from overuse, any redness or signs of an infection around its nonorganic components. The card reader could get disconnected. That sort of thing."

Tori gives a nervous nod. She imagines that all sorts of things could go wrong with it. The human body isn't supposed to be transformed into such a device. She assumes she'll be calling this number a lot.

The salesman continues, "But one thing that must be perfectly clear: you are not to purposely cause harm to The Darren II. If you damage it or neglect it in any way, there will be severe consequences. Although you should treat it like an exercise bike, if you abuse the machine it will be the same as abusing a human being. You could face fines and jail time. And if it dies you will likely be charged with murder."

Tori panics. "What? But what if it dies on its own? What if it has a heart attack? What if it's the fault of the surgery?"

The salesman nods. "If the machine dies the matter will be thoroughly investigated. You have no reason to worry as long as you don't mistreat it. Just be sure to call the emergency number if anything ever seems wrong with the bike and you'll be fine. If you break its leg or arm while exercising it will be completely understandable as long as you don't ignore the injury."

Tori takes a deep breath, but accepts full responsibility for the bike. She understands. If she were to be turned into a human exercise bike she would want to make sure her owner didn't neglect or injure her while in his care.

"So when do I get paid?" Tori asks.

The salesman smiles. "Thirty-five thousand in cash will be paid up front. You'll receive it with the bike on delivery. Then you'll receive fifteen thousand a month for the rest of the contract. If The Darren II is satisfied with the arrangement he might offer to extend the contract. Tips and gifts might also be awarded during or after the contracted period."

Tori gets to the last page of paperwork. Before she signs, the salesman puts his hand on the page and looks her in the eyes.

He says, "But one thing to keep in mind: once you sign this, you will not be able to break the contract. You must use The Darren II for a full year. If you want to cancel the agreement before the end of the period you will be forced to pay back the two hundred thousand in full within thirty days."

Tori takes a deep breath. She knows she shouldn't make this decision lightly. She knows she should take at least a week to think about it. She knows that she should just throw the pen at the man's face and walk out of there forever.

But before she can convince herself to change her mind, she signs her name on the dotted line.

The salesman grabs the paperwork and locks it in a safe, then explodes with excitement. He grabs Tori by the hand and shakes it furiously.

"Thank you," he cries. "Thank you so, so much."

There's almost tears in his eyes. Tori isn't sure if he is so excited because he's about to receive a very large commission for getting her to agree to take the bike or if he is just happy to be rid of the horrific machine that has been haunting the back storeroom for god knows how long.

# CHAPTER THREE

Tori instantly regrets the decision. She hits the car steering wheel as she drives home, calling herself stupid and weak for signing the agreement. Even with the money she'll be getting and the calories she'll be able to earn, she still doesn't want to have that monstrous creature in her home. Then she realizes that it's not too late. She can still get out of it. They haven't even paid her yet. Once the delivery people arrive at her house, she can just tell them to take it back. She doesn't want it anymore.

But then hunger stabs deep inside of her stomach. She cringes at the pain. It feels like her body is dissolving her from the inside out. Her fingers quiver against the steering wheel.

She contemplates her situation. Perhaps she can use the exercise bike for just a little while, just to get some extra calories. She won't spend any of the money. She'll just use it to get extra food. Then take it back whenever she wants. Or better yet, she can use the thirty-five thousand she'll get to buy another U-Fit machine and tell them to fuck off when they want their money back.

What can they do? It'll just be yet another debt she'll never be able to pay off.

When Tori gets home, her living room is filled with wasps. The insects have built an intricate maze of nests between the walls. She didn't realize they were there when she first moved into the apartment. Sometimes she heard buzzing sounds coming from behind her television, but never expected she was harboring thousands of insects behind a thin wall. They've probably lived there for years, coming in through an entrance on the roof or the outside wall. It wasn't until she hammered a quarter-sized hole that she realized what she was sharing her apartment with. Several small flying insects poured out of the hole and stung her on her arms and neck.

She tried calling the apartment manager, but nothing ever gets done about it. The woman who runs the office says she's allergic and refuses to go near them. She also won't be bothered to hire an exterminator and said just to plaster the hole to prevent them from getting inside.

Tori goes to the hole in the wall behind her plasma television and places a new layer of duct tape over the opening. She never plastered the hole—if that would even work—because she wants to have access to the wasps. Whenever she's short on calories, the wasps are her emergency food source.

"Guess I know what I'm eating tonight," she says to

the swarm of insects flying around her room.

She doesn't have the patience to eat them slowly. Usually, she savors each and every one, eating them alive while they're still buzzing inside her cheeks. But because so many of them got in this time, she plans to eat them by the bowlful.

With a fly swatter, she smacks them out of the air, smashes them against her couch or coffee table. Four of them sting her during the killing spree, but she's used to the pain. The venom feels pleasant in her bloodstream. Then she gathers them up in a cereal bowl and eats them with a spoon, gobbling them down ferociously, like it's been days since she's had anything. Their crispy exoskeletons taste a bit like popcorn. Their moist insides like savory lobster cream sauce.

When she's done with them, she hunts for any stragglers that might have been left behind. She feels like a feral cat as she swats at wasps landing on furniture and stuffs them into her mouth. She imagines how she might look if anyone were to see her. But she doesn't have a choice. The hunger is too overwhelming when she doesn't have enough calories. And the most shocking thing about it is how much she enjoys eating them. Hunger can make even the most repulsive food seem delicious.

The delivery men arrive at her front door and Tori smiles at them with sores on her gums. A wasp wing stuck to her upper lip.

The bearded delivery man standing in front stares at her sores like she's got some kind of horrible disease, but he doesn't say anything about it.

"Victoria Manetti?" he asks.

"Yes," she responds, then licks the wasp wing off of her lip. "Do you have it?"

He holds out a clipboard and has her sign for it.

Then the two men go to the back of the truck and pull out a large cardboard box that reads Darren II with a picture of the human bike on the side. Tori wonders why the hell they would design packaging for it. There's only one of these bikes in existence. She wonders if this is part of the man's fantasy. Perhaps he gets off on being treated as merchandise. Perhaps he wants to experience what it feels like to be opened like a product by its consumer.

A crowd of people gather outside of the apartment, admiring the U-Fit truck. They all seem jealous of Tori for being able to get herself a calorie-earning exercise bike. None of them notice The Darren II picture on the front of the box or they wouldn't be so envious.

"Where do you want it?" the bearded delivery man says as he enters the apartment.

"Downstairs in the office," Tori says.

They take the box down the steps into the office. There's hardly room for them to enter. Tori has been using it more as a storage space than an office. Boxes, old furniture, and clothes are stacked in high piles against the walls and spilling across the floors.

The bearded man looks back at Tori and says, "This

isn't going to work. The Darren II would rather be in the living room."

Before they can carry the box upstairs, Tori blocks the door and says, "I don't want it in my living room."

"The bedroom then," he says.

"No!" Tori nearly pushes him back to stop him from going toward her bedroom.

The guy looks at her with an annoyed expression. He doesn't like having to deal with the exercise bike any more than she does.

"I mean…" Tori says. "This is where I want it. It's going to be my exercise room. I just haven't set it up yet."

The bearded man sighs, but says nothing.

"Besides," Tori continues, "I was told not to give it special treatment. If I'm to treat it like a real exercise bike, then I want it in my exercise room. There's no place to put it in my living room. It might fit in my kitchen if I move my dining room table but that would be stupid."

The delivery man sighs again and looks down into his pocket.

He says, "The Darren II says that will be okay. Just make sure to clean this place up and make it nice. Put some mirrors in. Add a couple of yoga mats or other exercise equipment. Make it feel like a real exercise room."

Tori nods. "Sure."

The delivery men place the box on the ground and leave the room, turning off the light on the way out.

"We'll get the rest of the stuff," says the bearded man.

"What stuff?"

The delivery men don't respond. They go back to the

truck and return with six cardboard boxes with the U-Fit logo on them. The bearded man opens one of the boxes.

"This is its fuel," he says, pulling out a five gallon bucket and a hose. "You need to keep this in your refrigerator once it's opened."

"That?" she says, looking at the large container. "That thing won't fit in my fridge."

He ignores her and continues, "You feed it three cups of this daily." He holds up the funnel hose. "Put this in its feeding hole and just pour it in. You'll receive fifteen gallons a month. It will be plenty."

He points at two more boxes. They both read "Bike Food."

"Make sure to clean the hose before each feeding." He points at another box. "Cleaning equipment is in there. You can clean the bike once a week or whenever it... smells."

Tori cringes at the thought.

The delivery man opens the fifth box. "This is what you have to wear while using the bike."

He holds up a skimpy outfit that looks like a cross between something you'd exercise in and something a dominatrix might wear. It's a sleeveless leotard with a spandex hood. There isn't much of a lower half of the outfit. Just a crotchless G-string bikini that would leave very little protection between her genitalia and the bike seat while riding.

"I'm not wearing that!" Tori cries.

The delivery man speaks in a straight forward tone, without any remorse for her situation. "You have to. It's in your contract."

"But the crotch is wide open! My genitals will be rubbing all over that thing!"

The bearded man nods. "That's the point. You're also required to shave… You know, down there."

Tori holds up the outfit and winces. "I wasn't told about any of this."

"It's all in your contract," he says.

Tori shakes her head. "I can't do this anymore. Take all of this back. I won't be a *prostitute* for that freakish thing downstairs."

The delivery man shrugs. "I'm just paid to drop it off. You'll have to take that up with the U-Fit corporate office." Then he holds out his hand. "Let me see your phone."

She gives him her phone, thinking he's dialing the corporate office for her. But he's doing something else. Downloading something.

"Here's The Darren II app," he says, handing back her phone. "It reminds you when to exercise."

Tori holds out the phone to him. "No, you don't understand. I don't want any of this anymore. Call somebody and take this thing away."

"You'll have to handle that yourself. There's cancellation information in your user manual."

Tori groans, realizing the men aren't going to do anything to help her. She's stuck with the bike, at least for the night.

Before the men leave, Tori notices there is one box they delivered that was left unopened. She says, "What's in the last box?"

The bearded man looks back and says, "Open it and see."

Then he leaves her apartment, closing the door firmly behind him.

When Tori opens the box, she finds that it is filled with stacks of money. Thirty-five thousand dollars. They really paid her. Before she can get accustomed to holding that much money in her hands, she puts it back in the box, duct tapes it shut, and pushes it under her couch.

"There's no way I can go through with this," she says to herself.

A wasp lowers itself onto the tip of her nose. She shakes her head, curls her lips and blows at it, but the insect won't fly away until it finishes stinging the corner of her nostril.

# CHAPTER FOUR

Tori decides not to open the exercise bike. She plans to return it the next day, so she figures it would be best to just leave it in its box. But she finds it difficult sleeping in the room next to it. She swears she can hear it sneezing, clearing its throat, and shuffling inside the box. She wonders if it can suffocate in there. She wonders if she'll wake up to it dead in her office and be charged with criminally negligent manslaughter.

It's four in the morning and she still can't sleep. She goes into the office and turns on the light, staring at the box. Deep breathing issues from inside. The bike must be sleeping. Tori just stares at the box, examining the disturbing image of the man-bike on the exterior. The U-Fit logo is plastered on the front, with large text inside a pink bubble that exclaims, "Feel the burn!"

Tori tears at the corner of the box and then pulls it open. The sides of the box fall to the floor. When she sees the bike is covered in bubble wrap, she realizes what a mistake she's made. The bike must be suffocating. She unwraps it and tosses the bubble wrap aside. The plastic is soaking wet from bike sweat.

When the bike's eyes open and look at her, Tori realizes she's not dressed. The thing's eyes widen when it sees her bra and panties. She closes her robe and tightens it with her belt. Then she turns off the light and leaves the room. As she closes the door, she hears it gurgle and moan, as though begging her to ride it. But she has no intention of ever using the disgusting thing.

She goes upstairs and sleeps on the couch. Knowing the thing won't suffocate and is no longer within listening range, she's able to rest. Three hours later her alarm goes off, telling her that it's time to get up for work.

She takes the manual with her to work and calls the U-Fit corporate office, trying to figure out how to cancel her contract. They have no idea what she's talking about. She is put on hold several times and forced to wait. No matter how much she tries, she can't get anyone to help her remove the exercise bike from her property.

Without realizing it, she spends the bulk of her daily calories on snacks from the company vending machine at work. If she doesn't get more calories she'll be having carrot fries for lunch and wasps for dinner again. But riding The Darren II is not an option.

At lunch, she drives across town to a different U-Fit store and tries to buy a new exercise bike.

But the woman working there tells her, "I'm sorry

Miss Manetti, but we can't sell you anything here."

"Why not?" Tori asks.

"You're on a no-sell list," she says.

"What? Why?"

"I'm not sure," she says. "Have you ever committed any health crimes?"

Tori shrugs. "I once used a fake identity to get an extra calorie card."

The employee nods. "I see. That must be it. U-Fit doesn't sell equipment to people who might take advantage of the calorie system."

"But that was years ago," Tori says.

"I'm sorry. I can't sell anything to you. If you think this is in error, you'll have to contact the corporate office."

Tori doesn't argue any further. She knows what's happened. It has nothing to do with her criminal record. They won't sell Tori any exercise equipment because she is supposed to only use The Darren II. The bike doesn't want her using any other equipment but itself for the duration of the year.

By six o'clock p.m., Tori is starving and out of calories. But no matter what happens, she's not going to use The Darren II. She'll just eat more wasps. She'd rather eat nothing but wasps for the rest of her life than exercise on that sweaty monstrosity.

When she gets home, she runs into the office manager

outside of her apartment.

"What's going on, Mel?" Tori asks from her car window, concerned something might be wrong. She worries The Darren II might have been moaning so loud it upset the neighbors. Or perhaps she entered for yet another unscheduled walk-through and saw The Darren II for herself. Whatever it is, Mel never visits Tori unless it's because of a complaint or to annoy her in some way.

Tori exits her car and steps onto the sidewalk leading upstairs to her apartment. The manager waves and approaches her, holding a clipboard and wearing a stupid wool hat.

With a big dumb smile on her face, Mel says, "Hey, Tori. How's my favorite tenant?"

Tori hates Melanie. With her blond ponytail, peach-colored sweaters, and white plastic-framed glasses—she's like that third grade music teacher you hated as a kid. The one who was annoyingly happy and enthusiastic all the time, but was inflexibly cruel to any students who refused to laugh at her jokes.

"I'm fine," Tori says. "Is there a problem?"

"No problem," she says. "I hear you got a U-Fit machine."

So that's why she's there. Tori should've known.

"Uh, yeah," Tori says.

"Wow. I can't believe it. How did you afford it?"

Tori shrugs. "I saved up."

She tries to walk around the apartment manager, but the woman gets in her way.

"Can I see it?" Mel asks.

"I'm sorry. I'm really busy."

"I can come back later. Maybe at eight?"

Tori shakes her head.

But Mel continues, "I won't be long. I could really use the extra calories."

Tori groans. Of course that's what she's after. Before the health laws were put in place, Mel used to eat doughnuts, muffins, and cookies by the dozen. She's probably almost as desperate as Tori to get the extra calories.

"It doesn't work like that," Tori says.

"No, I know how they work," Mel says. "If I use my calorie card it will work just as good as yours. I just want a few hundred extra calories a week. That isn't asking too much."

Tori shakes her head. "I'm sorry. It's not going to happen."

She moves past her, but Mel follows her up the steps.

"I won't invade on your privacy, I promise. I can use it while you're at work. *Please.*"

Tori pulls out her keys and goes to her front door. "You don't understand. Only my card will work. It's a... *special* model. It's not like other U-Fit machines."

Mel says, "Well, what if I exercise on your card? You can buy me the food with the calories I earn."

Tori shakes her head as she opens the door. "I don't think so."

"I'll pay you," Mel says, sticking her foot in the door. "You'd make money and you don't even have to do any exercise. You can even keep any leftover calories I don't spend."

"You're asking me to do something illegal."

"It doesn't matter. It will be our secret."

Tori just shakes her head in response. Mel's face goes from desperate to fuming.

"You're so selfish!" Mel cries. "And after what I did for you today, I can't believe it!"

"Did what?"

"You didn't get my email? I finally got an exterminator out here to get rid of your wasp problem."

"You did what!" Tori's voice is so loud it forces Mel to take a step back.

Mel stutters for a second, then says, "I thought you'd be happy. You've been wanting me to do something about the wasps forever."

"They're dead? All of them?"

"Well, yeah. The whole hive was sprayed and removed. There was a ton of them, too. You should've seen it."

Tori slams her head into the wall.

"What?" Mel asks. "I thought you wanted them gone."

Tori sighs and says, "It's fine. Forget it."

"So can I use your U-Fit machine or not?"

"Not. And if I ever catch you breaking into my apartment when I'm not around, I'm calling the police."

Mel just gasps in shock at her response as Tori slams the door in her face.

As Tori steps into her living room, looking for any wasps that might have been left behind, a text comes onto her phone. It's from her exercise bike.

It reads:

> DARREN II: It's time to exercise! Are *you* ready to get *fit* with *U-Fit!*

Tori closes the message and tosses her phone on the couch. Then she searches her living room for wasps. She's sure some of them had to have survived. But after an hour of searching, she only finds a lone wasp perched on a copy of *Zen and the Art of Motorcycle Maintenance* on her bookshelf.

It's her last wasp, so she savors it. She presses it against her tongue. It buzzes and flaps. Its wings flitter against the side of her lip as it stings her gums. She puts it inside and sucks on it, allowing it to sting her again. She sucks the wings off its body and chews them with her front teeth, holding the rest of its body tightly inside her cheek. She doesn't kill it by biting. She pulls its body apart with suction, sucking its abdomen from its thorax and squishing it gently against the roof of her mouth until it explodes with creamy fluid. The insect dissolves in her saliva, crumbles into tiny pieces. When there isn't any more flavor to taste, she swallows the remains.

When it's finished, Tori can't believe how upset she is that she'll no longer be able to eat wasps whenever she wants. She hopes she'll be able to find a new wasp nest somewhere in the neighborhood.

Her phone buzzes as a new text comes in. She reads it.

DARREN II: Don't forget to shave your nether region. A smooth ride is a good ride!

Tori throws her phone back on the couch.

"Gross," she says, wiping her hands on her shirt as though she was just handling something dirty.

She wonders if there's anything in the contract against deleting the app that sends her those disturbing automated messages.

Tori doesn't plan to ride the exercise bike, but she realizes she'll still have to feed it. She doesn't want to get charged with neglect.

Carrying a five gallon bucket in one hand, the hose and measuring cup in the other, Tori goes downstairs to her office. When she turns on the light, she sees the exercise bike in the exact position it was left in last night. Just sitting there, breathing, shivering, waiting to be ridden.

Tori doesn't look the thing in the eyes when she feeds it. She unscrews a cap on its mouth, revealing a gaping wet hole. It's not much of a mouth anymore. The lips, teeth, tongue, uvula, tonsils, upper and lower jaws have all been removed, leaving only a direct opening to its throat. She rubs the hose with a jelly-like lubricant and inserts it into the passageway, then places a wide funnel on the end.

"Here it goes," she says, scooping a cup of Bike Food out of the five gallon bucket of black pudding-like syrup.

She pours the goop into the funnel and it slides slowly down the tube into its throat. The bike shivers and wheezes next to her as it is fed. Tori can feel the warmth issuing from its frame. It shifts side to side, leaning toward her arms as she feeds it, trying to feel her skin against its own. But as the bike inches closer, Tori inches way. She dumps the next two cups into the funnel before the first cup is finished going down, then holds the hose straight into the air as to make the fluid go down as quickly as possible.

The bike farts. Tori hears a high-pitched popping sound issue from its backside, but she doesn't realize what it is until the smell fills the room. It's like sour broccoli. She waves the odor away from her nose as the last of the bike food empties into the throat hole.

"Jesus Christ…" she moans.

Then she screws the lid back over the bike's mouth and takes the feeding supplies upstairs.

Opening the refrigerator, Tori has no idea how she's going to store a five gallon bucket inside of it. Though her fridge is empty of any real food, it is completely full of calorie-free items such as mustards and soda water. Whenever she's starving, she eats calorie-free food just to try to trick herself into thinking she's actually eating something. It sometimes takes the hunger away.

In order to fit the five gallon bucket inside, Tori has to remove all the shelves and pack as much food into the vegetable drawers as possible. She leaves out all the cans of soda water.

The act of digging in her refrigerator causes an instinctual reaction in her stomach. Hunger pierces her insides, forcing her to curl into a ball on her kitchen floor.

"Damn it," she cries, closing her eyes tight and squeezing her loose belly skin.

When the pain diminishes and she opens her eyes, Tori finds herself looking directly at the bucket of Bike Food. Her mouth waters. She realizes that the stuff must be loaded with calories. If three cups is all the exercise bike needs to survive it must be close to a hundred calories an ounce.

Tori sits up and does some math. The bike requires twenty-four ounces of the food a day, seven hundred and twenty ounces a month. It only needs a little over eleven gallons of food, leaving almost four gallons that would go to waste. Tori realizes she can eat this stuff. She doesn't have to starve.

Removing the lid and dunking the measuring cup into the black syrup, she tosses the bike food down her throat without even smelling it first. The feeling of something entering her stomach calms her, dissolves the hunger away. Her eyes relax. Her muscles go slack. But then she tastes it.

The fluid shoots out of her throat and sprays across the tile floor. The bike food isn't edible. It tastes of baby vomit mixed with motor oil, and it has a sour broccoli fart aftertaste. Tori pukes the rest of it into the sink. The stuff is horrid. It really is more like fuel than food. She'd rather eat doggy kibble than this crap.

She moans and drools at the flavor, squeezing half a tube of toothpaste on her tongue.

When the taste is finally gone and the bucket of food is hidden in her fridge, Tori realizes that the act of eating and puking only made her hungrier. She's not going to be able to sleep with these pains. She has to get more calories in her body. But the only way to earn calories is to use the exercise bike. If only she could earn calories without actually riding it.

Then she remembers the man she met at McDonald's. He said there was a device that could pedal U-Fit exercise bikes for her, earning calories without even having to touch it. If she uses that she'll be set.

Tori finds the piece of paper with the man's number written on it, hoping he'll be able to help her. She knows it's a long shot, but if she can get the device tonight she won't have to go to bed hungry.

The man picks up after three rings.

"Hello?" he asks.

"Is this Dave?"

He pauses, probably thinks she's some kind of telemarketer.

Then he says, "Yeah, who's this?"

"Tori. We met at McDonald's yesterday. Remember me?"

His voice changes from suspicious to cheerful. "Oh yeah, you're the girl who ate my broccoli. How's it going?"

Tori wheezes when he says *broccoli*. She doesn't want to think about broccoli ever again.

"It's going okay. I got a U-Fit exercise bike like you recommended, but I'm wondering about that device you were talking about. The one that pedals for you."

"Ah, yes. Right. I'll see what I can do to help you out, but we probably shouldn't talk about it over the phone. Want to meet me for dinner tomorrow?"

"How about tonight?"

"Well, I don't have any calories left to eat dinner tonight."

"Neither do I, but we don't have to eat anything. That's why I'm calling. I was hoping I could get one of those things as soon as possible, tonight if you can swing it. I'm starving."

"Uhhh…" Dave laughs as he thinks. "Well, I don't know if we'll be able to get you one tonight. But we can try."

"Great. That would be amazing."

"Meet me at the bowling alley on Barber," he says. "I'll call my guy and see what I can do."

"Sounds good. I'll head right over."

Tori ends the call. She grabs her car keys and the box of cash.

On the way out the door, she gets a text from her exercise bike.

> DARREN II: Don't forget to exercise tonight. It's never too late to get fit with U-Fit!

Tori deletes the text. If she ever finds out who's responsible for composing these automatic messages she's going to punch him right in the face.

When Dave meets her at the bowling alley, he's dressed in a nice button-up shirt and freshly ironed slacks. It's like he thinks they are going on a date.

The first thing he says is, "Want to bowl a few games?"

Tori looks back at the lanes, then back at him. "Uh, I don't really bowl. I didn't think that's what we were going to be doing."

He shrugs and puts on a smile. "Well, don't you think it'll be a little suspicious if we meet at the bowling alley without actually playing at least one game?"

Tori looks back at the lanes again. "I guess we can pay for a game, but don't expect much from me."

"It's okay. I'll give you some pointers."

As they check out pairs of bowling shoes, Tori wonders if this guy actually happens to have any connections at all. He could have just made the whole thing up to give her his phone number. He probably just wants to get into her pants.

They choose the most private lane on the end, far

away from the other bowlers.

As Dave chooses a sixteen pound ball, he says, "So I've got good news and bad news."

Tori looks over at him as she changes her shoes.

He says, "The good news is that we can get you a spinner tonight."

"Spinner?"

"That's what the device is called. A spinner." He steps closer to her, sticking his fingers into his ball to test the hole size. "But the bad news is that it's not cheap. It'll cost five grand."

Tori shrugs. "No problem."

"Seriously?" he asks.

"Yeah, I'm desperate. I'll pay pretty much anything for extra calories."

Dave smiles. "Well, in that case, put your shoes back on. We've got somewhere better to be."

"Where's that?"

"You'll see."

Then Dave rolls his ball down the lane and knocks over half the pins. He would have looked a lot cooler if he had gotten a strike.

# CHAPTER
# FIVE

They take Dave's truck across town. Tori has about ten grand in cash hidden in her coat. She's not sure about this guy or the place they're headed, but she feels it's worth the risk. Even if he turns out to be a crook who takes all her cash and leaves her on the side of the road, she doesn't care. It's not her money anyway.

"So where are we going?" Tori asks.

"We're going underground." He lights a black market cigarette.

"Underground?"

"The junk food underground."

"There's a junk food underground?"

"Prohibition didn't stop alcohol from being sold illegally. The health laws only created a booming criminal junk food market."

"You're kidding, right?" Tori asks.

"I heard the rumors, but I didn't know it was real until recently. They're supposed to have whatever you want to eat and not a single thing gets charged to your calorie card."

"Holy shit..." Tori says.

She realizes that she doesn't even need a spinner or an exercise bike. She can just buy food on the black market. A smile stretches across her face. It seems like a dream.

Then she says, "Do they have Big Macs?"

Dave laughs. "I wish. But they probably have cheeseburgers. *Real* cheeseburgers. I'm going to blow my whole paycheck at this place."

Tori pats the wad of cash in her pocket. "If this place is all you're saying it is then dinner's on me."

They arrive at what looks like a large office building hidden in a warehouse district near the river. There are no signs on the exterior of the building. No company logos. If it wasn't for all the cars in the parking lot Tori would have assumed the place was abandoned.

"This is it?" Tori asks.

"That's what my friend said," Dave says. "A big gray building with tinted windows."

"So what's inside?"

"A mall."

"A whole mall?"

"Yep. Full of vendors, restaurants, grocery stores, bakeries. You name it."

"How do the cops not know about this place?"

"Who says they don't? Cops eat junk food, too. Haven't you noticed how the cops in this town seem a lot fatter than anyone else? They probably get to eat whatever they want for free."

They park the car and head for the entrance. There's a line of people waiting to get in with four large bouncers in black suits guarding the door.

As they queue up, Dave leans toward Tori and whispers, "My friend says the password is *Salmon Pizza*. Tell them that if they ask."

While waiting in line, two large men are denied entry. They are each about three hundred pounds. Tori hasn't seen anyone with so much excess weight in years.

"No fatties," the bouncer says. "Come back when you lose some weight."

One of the fat men is ready to walk away, but the other stands his ground.

"What do you mean we're too fat?" says the angry fat man. "Do you know who I am?"

"I don't care who you are," the bouncer responds.

"I've spent more money here than any of your other customers combined. You have to let me in."

"Look, we can't let anyone in who is visually obese. Those are the rules. The feds see fat people walking around the city and they'll be forced to shut us down. If you really were a regular customer you'd already know that."

"Your boss is going to hear about this," the fat man says. "And when he hears you refused my business, you're going to wake up in a ditch somewhere."

"Whatever, Porky. Come back when you lose fifty pounds."

The fat men eventually step down and return to

their car, cursing and hollering at the tops of their lungs.

When it's Tori's turn to meet with the bouncer, he looks her up and down.

"Haven't seen you here before," the bouncer says. "You're way too skinny to be a regular."

"It's her first time," Dave says, stepping forward.

The bouncer holds up his hand so that Dave knows to stay back with the rest of the line.

"So what would you like for dinner?" the man asks.

Tori smiles and says, "I don't know. It depends on what's available. I'm pretty much up for anything, though. I'm starving."

The bouncer just stares at her.

Then he repeats himself. "No, I mean *what would you like for dinner?*"

Tori is confused. "I don't know. A cheeseburger maybe…"

The bouncer rolls his eyes and laughs. Tori wonders if wanting a cheeseburger is stupid. Perhaps they don't even have cheeseburgers in there.

"I'm asking for the password, lady," says the bouncer.

Then Tori understands the confusion.

"Oh. Of course. Salmon Pizza. That's what I'd like for dinner."

But after telling him the password, the bouncer still looks at her with an annoyed face.

"Okay, get lost," he says, then looks at Dave. "Next."

Tori panics. "But I just told you the password. Salmon Pizza. What's the problem?"

The bouncer sighs. "That was last week's password."

"Well, what's the new password?" Tori asks.

"If I told you then what would be the point of having a password in the first place? You obviously got the password from someone else, which means you're not a trusted customer. So get lost."

Tori just stares at the bouncer with her mouth drooped open. She's so close. She can't be turned away now.

Dave steps forward and says, "Come on, you've got to let us in. We just want a spinner. We'll be in and out in ten minutes."

The bouncer won't budge. He says, "Not my problem." Then waves them off.

Just before Tori steps out of line and walks away, someone steps toward the bouncer and says, "They're with me."

Tori looks back. It's a Sicilian man in his late fifties, wearing a designer gray suit, a manicured white goatee accentuates his prominent chin. When the bouncer sees him, he lowers his head.

"I'm sorry, Mr. Ferlisi," says the bouncer. "I had no idea they were with you."

Mr. Ferlisi steps toward him, placing a couple large bills into his coat pocket, then pats him on the shoulder. "It's my mistake. Thank you for understanding."

He opens the door to the building and waves Tori and Dave inside.

"After you," he says.

Tori and Dave say "Thank you" as they pass the Sicilian business man, but they don't stick around to introduce themselves to him. Once inside, they take off into the crowd of shoppers and don't look back.

"Who was that guy?" Tori asks Dave once they're at a safe distance.

"No idea," Dave says. "But he doesn't seem like the kind of guy you want to be friends with."

Tori nods her head. She doubts the man helped them out of kindness. At best, he wanted Tori to have dinner with him. At worst, he wanted more than just dinner. She just wants to get in and out before she attracts the attention of any other shady characters.

The place is even more extravagant than Tori imagined. It really is a mall of illegal junk food. Although it was once an office building, the offices have been transformed into small shops, selling anything from ice cream sundaes to fried potato chips to chipotle-injected Vienna sausages.

"Oh, wow," Tori says, staring at food carts lining the hallways.

The smells are even more beautiful than the sights. Buttered popcorn, Chicago-style hot dogs, fried chicken and potato wedges cooked in real animal fat. The scents are enough to make Tori's soul ooze out of her body and drift away.

"I was hungry before," Tori says. "But all this food is making me absolutely starving."

As they fight the crowd to get to a barbeque stand, Tori sees the price and her heart sinks in her chest.

"Shit…" Dave says.

The cost of a single cheeseburger is 2,000 dollars.

"That's a bit more spendy than I thought it was going to be."

Tori shakes her head. "I don't care. I'm getting one."

Dave pulls her back before she can order. "Let's keep looking. There might be cheaper stuff around. If they sell ground beef I'll make you a burger you'll never forget."

Tori nods.

Dave says, "Let's go find you a spinner first. After that, we can see what's available to eat."

Passing through the wonderland of deliciousness, Tori keeps her eyes on the price tags. Most things don't even have prices attached, meaning they are most likely too expensive to even consider unless you're so well off that money is no object. The cheapest food Tori can find is a chocolate truffle for three hundred dollars. The people who run this place are probably getting rich off of the new health laws. No way could anyone, even the most gourmet upscale restaurant, get away with charging two thousand for a cheeseburger before the laws were passed.

"Spinners," Dave says, pointing at an office turned U-Fit store.

He leads Tori into the store and greets a short man with a beer belly and plaid scarf at the door. The guy doesn't seem to have shaved or showered in several days. Scraggly facial hair grows in patches across his cheeks and neck.

"We're looking for a spinner," Dave says.

"Sure," the man says, speaking soft and slow like

he's been smoking opium all night. "Come this way."

He takes them into the store, filled with black market exercise machines and other equipment. Unlike the other shops in the underground mall, this one is the least flashy. It doesn't seem to cater to the upper class clientele like the rest of the mall. The machines sold here are for people who can't afford the normal U-Fit equipment available in stores. It also looks like they don't work as well, like the guy picked up a bunch of half-broken machines from the Goodwill and attached U-Fit card readers on them.

"Here's all the spinners I got," he says, pointing at a row of cardboard boxes with small cylindrical machines in them.

Then he plops down on a well-worn couch and lights a bong.

Tori looks at the closest one. "How much?"

The short guy waits until he exhales three smoke rings before he answers. "For you? I'll give you a deal. How's ten thousand sound?"

"I thought they were five thousand?" Tori says.

The guy shrugs. "You thought wrong."

"Well, ten thousand's all I've got. How am I supposed to get dinner?"

The guy puts down his bong and holds up a small tin foil package. "I'll throw in this pot brownie for free if you want."

"Does it even work?" Dave asks.

The short guy isn't as pleasant with Dave as he is with Tori. "Of course it works. You think I'd stay in business with faulty merchandise?"

# EXERCISE BIKE

Tori points at one of his exercise bikes. "Can I try it out?"

The guy shrugs. "Go for it." Then he returns his mouth to the bong.

Tori and Dave take one of the spinners out of its box, then spend a few minutes trying to figure out how it works. There's a clamp that attaches to the right bike pedal. Tori inserts her calorie card into the card reader, then flips a switch on the spinner. The bike pedals itself, adding calories onto her card. She shifts a lever upward and the spinner speed increases, peddling the bike at thirty miles per hour.

After ten minutes, Tori already has two hundred calories. Much more than she would earn peddling an exercise bike the normal way. She turns off the spinner and retrieves her calorie card.

"I'll take it," she says.

The short guy doesn't seem to care either way. "Great…"

Tori drops several stacks of cash onto the table next to the store owner's bong. Then she grabs the foil-wrapped pot brownie and leaves the store.

"Well, I'm broke," Tori says. "I guess I won't be eating a cheeseburger after all."

Dave pats her on the back. "I'm sorry about that. My friend must not be as connected as he claims to be."

"It's okay. I'll come back another time."

"Next time I get a password, I'll make sure it's legit."

As they pass a gyro stand, Tori drools over the spinning lamb meat. She inhales the greasy scent as deep as she can. Because she's so hungry, her sense of smell is heightened. The aroma is so strong it's almost as though she's tasting it.

"This place is like heaven," Tori says, trying to tear her eyes away from the gyro meat as they pass.

Dave nods. "A really, really expensive heaven."

"So you wouldn't happen to have enough money to buy us dinner, would you?" Tori asks.

He shakes his head. "Uh, I can afford a candy bar. Maybe. But I'd rather not. I had no idea how much everything was going to cost here."

"Well, let's just walk around for a while. Just smelling all this stuff is better than anything I've eaten in a year."

As they walk past an Italian restaurant, Tori and Dave find themselves slowing down to a stop. They peer through the windows like two stray dogs begging for scraps. The smell of Italian meats and cheeses serenades them into a trance. Just watching the food as it's eaten by wealthy upper class citizens brings a smile to Tori's face. They serve real meatballs, real sausages. The mozzarella isn't dairy-free. The pasta isn't gluten-free. The wine is well-aged and full-bodied, not that watered-down Diet Wine crap they sell in stores now. And not a single dessert on the menu is chia pudding.

"I'm eating here tomorrow," Tori says. "I don't care

how much it costs. I'm eating here."

"Count me out," Dave says. "I bet eating here costs two year's income."

Saliva builds in Tori's mouth. "Totally worth it."

A familiar face peeks out of the restaurant entrance at Tori.

"Admiring my fine establishment?" he asks.

It's the Sicilian man they met outside. He steps out of the restaurant and approaches them.

"You rushed away so quickly I didn't get a chance to introduce myself," he says.

He only looks at Tori as he speaks, completely blocking Dave out of his line of vision. It's as though he doesn't even hear his voice when Dave says, "Sorry, we were in a hurry."

"I am Federico," he says, grabbing hold of Tori's hand. He doesn't shake it, just holds it firmly in the air.

"My name is Tori," she says, putting on a fake smile. "Tori Manetti."

"Ah, a beautiful name," he says. "You're not related to a Vincent Manetti are you?"

Tori shakes her head. "No, who is he?"

"Nevermind," Federico says. "Would you by any chance be interested in sampling a little of my menu?"

Tori's eyes open. "Are you kidding me?"

Federico nods. "It would be my pleasure to feed you. No charge." He glances at Dave for the first time. "You can even bring your little puppy dog with you."

Before Dave can object, Tori says, "Of course I would. I'm starving."

"Aren't we all?" he says with a smile.

Federico leads her toward the restaurant entrance.

"Tori, I think we should go," Dave says.

She just glares at him. "I'm sorry, but there's no way I'm passing this up."

Federico looks at Dave. "Come. I insist."

Dave reluctantly follows.

# CHAPTER SIX

Federico leads them through the restaurant and into a large kitchen in the back. Several chefs work furiously to cook for the hungry crowd in the dining hall. Every one of them was probably a top chef before the health laws were passed. Every one of them probably makes ten times what they did back then.

He takes a small appetizer plate right from the hands of one of his cooks and holds it out to his guests.

"Stuffed mushroom?" he asks, popping one of them into his mouth.

Dave and Tori taste one each. When Tori bites into it, the sizzling ball explodes in her mouth, filling her with buttery goodness. She hasn't tasted anything as delicious. The breading, the sausage, the seasoning. They don't legally make food like this anymore. Not anywhere.

"Good?" Federico asks.

The two of them just nod and moan with pleasure as they savor every particle in their mouths.

Federico looks at one of the chefs. A large man with a thick chin. He says to him, "Marco, prepare the private room for my two guests here. Give them anything they want from the menu. On me."

The large chef nods and then goes through a door at the end of the kitchen.

Tori's eyebrows rise up her forehead. "Oh, thank you. You're a godsend."

"Of course," he says. "You two should enjoy yourselves. Food such as this is to die for."

Dave laughs. "I used to eat food this good all the time. Fucking health laws ruined everything…"

As the words escape his mouth, Dave immediately regrets saying it. Federico looks at him with utter contempt.

"Those health laws have made me a rich man," Federico says. "I couldn't be happier with them."

Dave stands there uncomfortably for a moment. He looks back at Tori. She squeezes the spinner box tight to her chest.

They both jump when Federico claps his hands together. "But enough politics. The room is surely ready for you." He gestures toward the door. "Go ahead."

Dave takes Tori by the hand and leads the way. She doesn't know why Dave is being so protective. He's acting more like a boyfriend than a strange guy she barely knows. He's not really her type anyway. Not that Federico is any better. If she had to choose, she'd probably go with the Sicilian all the way. At least he'd keep her well-fed.

"I don't know about you, but I'm ordering everything on the menu," Tori says, giggling with excitement.

Dave smiles. "All I want is a steak. A big, fat juicy slab of beef."

As he opens the door and steps into the room, he looks back at Tori and gives her a wink. Then the large chef yanks him inside and slices his throat open with the blade of a butcher knife.

It isn't a private dining room, prepared just for them. The room is designed for one purpose: butchering animals. And judging by the bones in the large bins lining the wall, it isn't just cows and pigs they slaughter here.

Tori screams as Federico shoves her inside and locks the door behind him. Blood gushes out of Dave's neck as he drops to the floor. He jerks three times before his body goes limp, his pool of blood indistinguishable from the rest of the fluids that already coated the floor.

"I'm so very sorry about this, Miss Manetti," Federico says, straightening his tie.

The large chef grabs her and forces her into a blood-stained chair in the center of the room.

"Unfortunately, running a fine establishment such as mine comes with its unfortunate drawbacks. For instance, obtaining quality meat is not what it used to be. These days, the demand greatly outweighs the supply."

He steps toward her, rubbing his finger down her cheek as the chef holds her in place.

"We order all we can from South America, Asia, Russia, the Middle East…" He puts his finger in his mouth, tasting Tori's sweat. "But it's not always enough.

We can only get so much at a time. I'm sorry to say, but our supply is short this week. And we have a whole lot of customers paying top dollar to eat real, authentic Italian meats."

Tori struggles, but the chef is strong. He holds her down. He must weigh four times as much as she does.

Federico taps Dave's dead body with his designer shoe.

"Your friend here will have to be made into meatballs," he says.

Then he goes back to Tori and leans down, inches away from her face, and smiles at her. "And you're going to make the most delicious Italian sausages we've ever served."

"You sick fuck," Tori says.

He doesn't respond to her words, just smiling in her face.

She isn't sure if it's the smell of Italian meat cooking in the kitchen, the stabbing pains in her stomach, or all the talk of cannibalism, but something changes inside of Tori. While looking at the Sicilian man's face, examining every pore in his skin, smelling his musky sweat, salivating at his wet tongue as it licks his lips, a deep hunger overwhelms her body. They say that hunger raises all your senses, makes you think clearer, act faster. It all goes back to when we were hunters and gatherers, when hunger drove us, made us strong enough to catch our prey.

"I think I'll eat you with linguine and alfredo," he says, then bursts into a deep laughter.

He laughs right in her face, watching her squirm helplessly in the chair, knowing she's going to be turned into food and eaten by the city's elite citizens within the hour.

But his laughter is cut short as Tori bites his nose off.

Federico doesn't seem to realize what's happened to him at first. Just standing there, his mouth wide open. Then blood pours down his cheeks. He sees the chunk of meat in Tori's mouth as she chews it, savoring it just as much as she did the stuffed mushrooms only moments before.

He screams and leaps back as Tori goes in for another bite. Her teeth snap together an inch from his white-haired chin.

He feels for his nose, but only finds blood and bone in its place.

"You fucking bitch! You ate my nose!"

He pulls a gun from his coat and fires madly at her. But with Tori's heightened senses mixing with newfound adrenalin, she ducks down and the bullets perforate the large chef behind her.

In too much pain to aim properly, the Sicilian sprays bullets across the room. He slips on Dave's blood and falls back. Tori doesn't even think before she acts. As Federico tries to get up, she grabs the spinner from its cardboard box and slams it into his skull. His head cracks against the tile floor and he goes limp.

Tori takes the gun and gets to her feet. Shaking and jerking as she points the gun around the room. But there's no one left in there to hurt her. Just three motionless bodies lay on the ground.

As Tori steps out of the butcher room covered in blood, she fires the gun into the air. The other chefs run out of the kitchen. The patrons in the restaurant duck under the tables or run out into the mall.

"You know they've been feeding you human flesh here, don't you?" she yells at the cowering upper class restaurant customers. They stare at her with quivering eyes, probably not even hearing her slurred, crazy speech. "You stupid cannibalistic fucks!"

Before the security can get to her, she runs out of the mall, firing the gun in the air until it's out of bullets. Then she holds up the spinner like she's going to bludgeon to death anyone who gets in her way.

They let her go. Probably didn't figure out what she did until she was already gone. She walks all the way back to the bowling alley where she left her car. Even though she's covered in blood, nobody stops to ask her what happened. Not even the cops.

They killed Dave. They were about to kill her. But the worst part of it all, Tori is still hungry as hell. She'll never be able to return to the underground mall. Never be able to taste any of that heavenly junk food. The only thing she got out of it was this spinner. She hopes it didn't break when she slammed it into Federico's skull. If the spinner doesn't work anymore then all of it would've been for nothing.

When she gets home, Tori takes off her clothes and jumps into the shower, trying to wash all the blood away.

She wonders if anyone will hunt her down after what she did. Only Federico knew her name and he's dead. Or at least Tori thinks he's dead. She didn't check to make sure. If she only knocked him out and he survives, he'll come after her for sure. She probably won't be so lucky next time. The Sicilian prick will probably turn her into sausages for sure.

She tries to forget about it. There's nothing she can do. He either comes for her or he doesn't. In the meantime, Tori plans to earn as many calories as she can and eat like a king every meal of every day. It'll have to be health food, legal food, but at least there's no chance of accidentally consuming human flesh.

# CHAPTER SEVEN

Tori is still starving, but it's so late and she's so tired. Even if she could earn enough calories to eat something, she doesn't think she's up for going out. Pizza places aren't open as late as they used to be, back before they stopped selling pies with real meat and dairy. Most people don't have any calories left late at night, so businesses don't bother staying open. They do open much earlier than before. All restaurants open at 6am, which is when everyone's calorie cards reset for the new day. But Tori has no plans of staying up until six. Instead, she plans to hook the spinner up to the exercise bike and have it go all night, earning hundreds or even thousands of calories while she sleeps. Then in the morning she'll have the biggest feast she's had in years.

Tori cleans off the spinner and examines it for damage. It doesn't seem broken on the outside, but she isn't sure if any mechanical components have been shaken loose or not. Only thing to do is test it.

The exercise bike is asleep when she enters her office. She tries not to wake it while connecting the spinner to its right pedal. She inserts her calorie card, moving as quietly as she can. Then she turns on the spinner and pushes the speed up all the way to maximum. As the bike wakes, she turns off the light and exits the room before it notices her, leaving it spinning at full speed.

She goes to sleep on the couch upstairs, blocking the sound of spinning below her. The events of that night fade from her mind and are replaced by dreams of Black Bean Big Macs and Soyrizo Scrambles and all the other calories she'll be able to consume. Her diet is about to become so much more satisfying.

When Tori wakes, it feels like Christmas morning. She imagines the size of the breakfast she's going to have. With all the calories she's earned, she will just go from restaurant to restaurant, eating the biggest meal they have on every menu. Her stomach howls with excitement. She's never been so happy to be this hungry.

She calls in sick. Work will just get in her way. Her plans for the day consist of eating and more eating. Besides, after what she went through last night she deserves some time off.

Tori rushes downstairs and throws open the office door. The spinner roars at her. She doesn't care that she's wearing only her underwear. The bike is facing the wall, its eyes can't turn in her direction. It can't see her mostly naked body.

The thing isn't asleep. With all the spinning, it probably didn't get much sleep at all during the night. Tori doesn't really care. The pervert can sleep all day once she gets her calorie card.

When she looks at the screen displaying her calories, she doesn't understand what it means. It reads: -3264. The number just goes up from there as the pedals spin.

"What the fuck?"

She turns off the spinner, then looks at the calories again. It's stopped at -3269. Does she have negative calories? Is it even possible to get negative calories? She should have over 6000. It doesn't make sense.

"You've got to be kidding me…"

She wonders if the spinner was rotating backwards. Would her calories go down if she rides the bike backwards? That doesn't make sense. She'd still burn calories by peddling in reverse.

"Piece of shit."

She tosses the spinner across the room and then goes upstairs. She gets dressed, gets in her car, and goes to the convenience store down the road. When she tries to buy a granola bar, her fear becomes real.

"I'm sorry, but you don't have enough calories for this," the clerk says.

"Are you sure?" Tori asks.

He nods. His expression is as confused as Tori's was when she first saw it. "In fact, you've got… a large calorie deficit."

"How is that possible?"

He shrugs. "I have no idea. I've never seen this before.

Did you break a health law or something? Try to cheat the system? That's the only thing I can think of."

When he returns the card, Tori curses under her breath and drives back home. She realizes the spinner had to have done this. The Darren II is a more advanced machine than other U-Fit equipment. It can't be cheated like the other exercise bikes. Perhaps even its human brain is able to control the calorie intake, reporting when it is being used improperly.

Either way, Tori is fucked. Not only is the spinner useless, but she has a huge calorie deficit. She's lost the 2000 calories she was supposed to get for today, plus the bulk of tomorrow's calories.

As she pulls into her parking spot, it dawns on her... She can feel her heart sink in her chest. A thick ball of morning saliva gulps down her throat.

There's only one way she'll be able to get enough calories to eat that day.

She has no choice but to ride the exercise bike.

Tori has a long way to go just to get rid of the calorie deficit on her card. She doesn't waste any time, doesn't give herself a chance to think about what she's doing. She puts on thick pants, gloves, and a long robe. She places headphones over her ears and blasts Kylie Minogue with the volume all the way up. She covers the exercise bike with towels so that she doesn't have to see the grotesque thing as she rides it.

After inserting her calorie card, she gets onto the bike, closes her eyes tight, and starts peddling. Even with all the clothes she wears, she can't imagine it as a real bike. It feels like she's on an anorexic horse. Its weight shifts from side to side. She can feel it breathing beneath her. But she just clenches her teeth and keeps peddling.

Ten minutes of exercise and then she opens her eyes. She looks at the card reader to see how much of the deficit she removed. But the number is still going in the wrong direction.

"Fucking hell," she yells, tearing off the headphones.

Tori gets off the bike and looks at the screen, wondering what's going on. Perhaps it's not the spinner that subtracted the calories. Perhaps the card reader is just broken. She goes upstairs and gets the emergency number. If the bike is broken she needs to get it fixed.

As she turns on the phone, she sees a new text message.

DARREN II: Don't forget to wear your exercise outfit. You can't get fit without proper workout attire!

Tori lowers the phone. She realizes it's not that the card reader is broken. It's that she's not wearing the stupid fetish outfit that came with the bike.

"God damn it…"

Her plan to wear thick clothes isn't going to work. She has no choice but to wear the skimpy spandex slut suit.

She removes her clothes and takes the thing out of the box. It's hardly clothes at all. After she puts it on, she looks in a mirror and sighs. A draft hits her bare butt cheeks and covers them in gooseflesh. Her crotch is so uncovered that she could pee in a toilet and not even need to take the thing off.

Returning to the bike, she rides for a few more minutes. But the calories still move in reverse.

"Are you fucking with me?"

She removes the towels from the bike, staring down at its hairy pimpled bike-shaped flesh. Then rides some more and loses more calories.

"Don't fuck with me!"

Then she remembers. She's supposed to shave. The fucking perverted bike-thing doesn't want her pubic hair rubbing against it.

She goes into the bathroom, takes off her outfit, and brings a pair of scissors to her pubes. Once it's trimmed down as short as she can get it, she uses a pink disposable razor, showers off, and returns to the bike.

"This better fucking work," she says.

She gets on and pedals three times. The deficit is reversed by one point. Tori steps off the bike and walks out of the room.

"Finally!" she cries.

Then she hits the wall in relief. At least now she knows what the problem was. At least she can finally earn back calories. But after so many failed attempts, Tori isn't quite up for exercising just yet.

She goes upstairs, steps out on the balcony with a can of carbonated water in her hand, and then groans out all of her frustration. She just needs a quick break, has to mentally prepare herself for the disturbing experience she's about to go through. She thought she could beat the exercise bike. She thought she could cheat it, earn calories without playing its sick game. But she was wrong. The bike is going to get its way.

"This is going to suck…"

She closes her eyes and takes in a deep inhalation of fresh air. As she exhales, she opens her eyes to see Melanie, her apartment manager, on the street below. Melanie just stares up at her in shock.

Tori waves, standing there casually in her crotchless spandex outfit, her freshly shaved vulva basking in the sunlight for everyone to see.

Melanie awkwardly waves back and then walks on.

Once she's built up the courage, Tori marches downstairs to the exercise bike. Its flesh quivers with anticipation as she touches it. Gray hairs stand on end as her fingers rub the handle. When she straddles it, the fleshy seat is warm against her crotch. She puts her feet onto the bike's pedal-shaped feet, grips its handle-shaped arms, then starts riding.

It's difficult to see it as a piece of exercise equipment. The thing is too much of a living being. She can feel its bones through its skin as she squeezes the handles. It pulses and breathes between her thighs. It moans at the pleasure of being ridden. Although its mouth is lipless and covered with a lid, she can sense it smiling at the experience.

Tori tries to zone it out, she stares down at the bike, focusing in on its flesh. Its skin is covered in moles and liver spots. She pedals faster, trying to eliminate her calorie deficit as quickly as possible.

After an hour of riding, sweat drips down its frame, pooling in her crotch. The seat becomes slippery. Her buttocks slide back and forth as she pedals. The more she moans from the intense workout, the more the bike moans with her.

The penis at the end of the seat becomes erect as her crotch rubs against its base. She tries inching away, moving as far back on the seat as she can, but the sweat keeps sliding her back toward it. She pedals faster, her muscles burning. Because she's always had such a high metabolism, she's never needed to do much exercise to keep in shape. So she's quickly drained. Her muscles cramp up. Her heart pounds in her chest.

When Tori looks down, she is sprayed with the bike's ejaculate. It squirts white goo against her thighs, shooting all over the floor and bike frame. As the creamy warmth pools between her legs, she screams and jumps off the bike. It continues ejaculating as she steps away.

"What the fuck…" she cries.

Once it's finished, the bike lets out a long sigh. Its muscles relax. It closes its eyes in deep satisfaction.

"Fuck this," Tori says, running out of the room.

She still has the bulk of her calorie deficit to get through, but after that she can't continue riding it.

Nobody told her the thing would be coming all over her as she rode. This arrangement keeps getting worse.

Tori puts on some real clothes and leaves the house. She just has to get out of there for a while, take a walk, get some fresh air. Perhaps there's some fruit trees in the neighborhood she can plunder.

She doesn't find any fruit trees, but there are spiders. Spider webs line the manicured shrubs outside of her apartment complex. Using a long twig, she scoops a spider out of its web, crushes it against a rock so that it won't bite her while she eats it. Then she licks up the remains and moves on to the next arachnid.

Two children walking home from school see her in the bushes playing with spiders.

They just stare at her, amused by an adult doing the kinds of things kids like to do.

"What are you doing?" asks one of them, a little boy.

Tori responds in a casual voice. "Catching spiders."

The boy nods as though he completely understands.

"What kind of spiders?" he asks.

"Green ones and red ones," Tori says, coiling her twig around a web as its spider tries to climb away.

The little girl stays back, obviously nervous the spider might land on Tori's hand. She doesn't say anything but *oh* and *eww*.

The boy says, "Is it a comb-footed spider?"

"What's a comb-footed spider?"

"It's like a black widow, but not as poisonous. There's one in my bedroom window at home. It's big and red."

When the spider climbs onto the twig, Tori pulls it from the web. "Really? Aren't you scared it will get you?"

The boy shakes his head. "Dad says they eat bad bugs and won't leave their webs. Even though it can bite you, it's a good spider to have around."

Tori holds out the spider toward the little boy. His sister hides behind him. "Is this a comb-footed spider?"

The boy looks carefully. "No, that's just a garden spider."

"Are they poisonous?" Tori asks.

"No."

Tori nods. "Good." Then she puts the end of the twig in her mouth and pulls the spider off with her teeth.

As she chews the spider in her mouth, both of the children back away. Their mouths widen. They don't say anything else to her. When she turns back to the bushes, the children run away as fast as they can.

After she's eaten all of the spiders on the block, Tori gives up. They only made her hungrier. She'll never be able to collect enough bugs to meet her caloric needs.

The day is not turning out at all like she imagined it would. No all-day feast. No limitless supply of calories. It's the exact opposite of Christmas morning.

She sits down in the shade and rests her chin on her knees. A wave of depression spreads over her. The whole situation seems hopeless. She knows she's going to have to go back to her apartment and use the exercise bike again. It's really the only way.

A wasp lands on her arm and stings her three times. She grabs it and puts it in her mouth, chewing languidly. The flavor just isn't the same as it was when she had her own hive in her walls. Another wasp stings the back of her neck and she smacks it and licks up its remains. The sensation does nothing for her. Even eating wasps isn't enough to cheer her up.

As more wasps circle her head, she realizes a hive must be nearby. She searches the tree above her until she finds it. Then she goes back to her apartment, grabs a pillow case, and captures the hive. She receives dozens of stings on her face and arms, but it's totally worth it. She brings it back to her apartment and transplants it into her wall, hoping there's no lingering poisons from the extermination of the last wasp nest.

But even with new wasps in her house, everything still feels hopeless. There's nothing to do but go back to the exercise bike and gain all of her calories back. She just stares at the new hole in her wall, now ten times the size it used to be, fifteen pieces of duct tape over the opening. She lets out a loud sigh and then changes back into her exercise suit.

# EXERCISE BIKE

Bringing the box of cleaning supplies downstairs, she wipes down the bike's frame, cleaning the sweat and ejaculate from the seat. But just as she finishes washing the thing off, a brown ooze leaks out of its rear end.

"Are you serious?"

She steps back and watches as the thing shits all over itself and the carpet. The room fills with the scent of sour broccoli. Dark brown sludge boils out of it like baby shit.

"Can you get any more disgusting?" she asks the bike.

It's the first time she's ever spoken directly to the thing. When she steps in front of it, she sees the thing's eyes closed tight.

"I have to clean up your shit now, too?"

The bike is obviously humiliated, can't look her in the eyes. She just groans at it until it finishes going to the bathroom. Then she cleans up its mess.

"If you're going to shit, do it *before* I wash you," she says. "And don't even think about doing it while I'm riding you. Don't even fucking fart."

If she's going to be riding this thing every day from now on, she realizes she'll have to start cleaning it before she uses it and then feed it after she's done. It needs to get on a regular feeding schedule so it doesn't crap all over her while she's riding. When she's finished, she puts a bucket down below its anus.

When she notices the thing's penis is erect again, most likely getting turned on for being humiliated and chastised by her, she says, "Fucking pervert."

Tori sprays down the room with air freshener and lights some cinnamon candles. Then she puts on her headphones and gets back to exercising. She's not in the mood to deal with the bike's crap anymore. She'll just block him out and ride it as hard as she can until she either gets her calories back or breaks both its legs.

Its erection does not fade as she rides it. Its penis only gets harder. She ignores it, staring straight ahead, counting down the calories with every mile she rides.

*It's just an ordinary bike*, she says in her head. *Just an ordinary bike...* She looks down. *...with a penis.*

The bike's cock smacks against her thighs as she rides, but she doesn't stop. Even if the thing ejaculates all over her she won't stop riding. She needs to get her calories back even if she has to ride the thing all day.

Her crotch and G-string are soaked in sweat. She can't tell whether it's her own sweat or the bike's. Her labia rubs against the moist fleshy seat, almost stimulating her as she pedals. Riding the living exercise bike is not in the least bit erotic to her, but her body seems to be getting aroused. The thought disgusts her. She's not quite sure, it could just be from all the sweating, but it feels as though she's getting wet. Vaginal fluids mix with the bike sweat, forming an even more lubricated surface.

When Tori looks down, she observes something she didn't notice before. The bicycle is ribbed and bumpy. There is a pulsing vibration beneath the flesh. It's as though the seat was designed to sexually pleasure the woman riding it. Tori grinds her teeth and rides faster, ignoring the sensation between her legs.

She closes her eyes, focuses on the music in her headphones, trying not to put too much of her weight on the seat, trying not to become stimulated. No matter how sexual of an experience it is for the bike, she won't let it be that way for her. But with her eyes closed, her sense of touch becomes greater. She realizes that the seat can move beneath her. It wraps itself around her crotch like a giant slug, sliding against her clitoris.

Losing herself in the music, she is able to take her mind off of the sensations between her legs. But just as her mind wanders off and she forgets what is happening, something pushes itself inside of her.

She looks down to see the penis has somehow achieved penetration. She screams as her bike fucks her from below, the seat thrusting itself quickly in and out. Before she can jump off, the bike comes inside of her.

"Motherfucker!" she yells at the top of her lungs.

Then she kicks it over. The bike falls into a pile of boxes. Clothes, picture frames, and candles topple over on top of it. She kicks it again.

"What the fuck do you think I am? Your fucking whore?"

She stomps on the bike as it whimpers and whines, quivering on the floor.

"You're gone," she says. "I don't care about the money or calories. I'm getting rid of you. And if the store won't take you back I'm tossing your ass in the fucking garbage."

# CHAPTER EIGHT

Tori tries to wash the cum out of her with scalding hot water. If she had enough calories to buy a bottle of vodka she would have downed the whole thing in one sip.

"This is it. They're going to get it."

Tori doesn't just plan to return the exercise bike. She plans to sue the hell out of U-Fit for what just happened to her. She'll demand far more than the two hundred thousand she was promised. She'll also demand new exercise equipment, real exercise equipment, the kind she can use her spinner on. She'll never have to deal with The Darren II ever again.

But when she goes to the U-Fit store, they have no idea what she's talking about. A female salesman sees Tori in her panicked, angry state and thinks she's some kind of crazy person. She's obviously not dressed like someone who would shop at U-Fit.

"I've never heard of a Darren II model of exercise bike," she says.

"It was a *special* model. There was only one in existence. You *have* to know what I'm talking about. You had a special room in the back just for it."

The woman says, "There's only overstock stored back there. No special models. We only sell what's on the showroom floor."

"It is back there. I'll show you."

To humor Tori, the saleswoman takes her into the back. But the room isn't there anymore. The tinted window is gone. When she opens the door, there are only boxes of bike parts in the room. They look as though they've been there for a long time.

"I'm not crazy," Tori says.

The saleswoman looks at her as though she's not so sure. With swollen wasp stings all over her face, Tori looks like some kind of crazed meth addict.

"You should have my contract on file," Tori says.

The woman goes behind the register and looks it up, but there's no sign that a Victoria Manetti ever purchased a U-Fit bike.

"What about the man who worked here?" Tori asks. "He'll know what I'm talking about."

Tori describes what he looks like. A thin bald man, about six inches shorter than the saleswoman.

"There's no one by that description who works here," the saleswoman says.

"But he *did* work here," Tori says. "I know he did. Are you sure? How long have you worked here?"

"I've only been here for a year, but I know everyone who works at this location. The only man who works at this location is the boss, but he's six feet tall and has a full head of blond hair."

Tori squeezes her fists. "Well, you have to do something. I want that bike out of my house."

"I'm sorry, but if it's not a U-Fit bike from this location we can't pick it up. Are you sure you didn't buy it from another company?"

"Of course I'm sure."

The saleswoman shakes her head. "I'm sorry, but I can't help you."

Tori slams her hands onto the counter and yells, "But you have to help me. I can't take it anymore. I need it removed."

The saleswoman backs away. As Tori glares into her eyes, the woman suddenly feels in danger.

"I'm sorry, but I'm going to have to ask you to leave," she says.

But Tori only gets angrier. She yells, "Call your boss! Call corporate headquarters! I'm not leaving until somebody gets rid of that thing!" Then she breaks down in tears. Her emotions are going crazy. She doesn't know if it's because of all she went through or if it's the lack of food in her system, but she cries out loud, hardly able to speak.

"The bike raped me…" Tori says. "How would you like it if you were raped by your exercise bike!"

The saleswoman is convinced Tori must be on drugs. "It's just an exercise bike."

"No, it's not. It's a man. It's a human being who was turned into an exercise bike."

"I'm calling security," the woman says.

But Tori doesn't stick around for the mall security

to come after the saleswoman dials the number. She just screams in the lady's face, pushes a stack of paperwork off of the counter, and then kicks over a stair-climber on her way out.

Tori spends the next few days in a hotel. She calls the U-Fit emergency number and tells them that she's not at home and won't feed their disgusting bike-thing. She tells them she wants the bike gone. She wants the contract ripped up. If they don't want the bike to die, they have to go and get it themselves. Then she tells them she plans to sue the hell out of them for what the bike did to her.

But she doesn't actually get a human on the line to say all this to. It's just an automated system. She leaves message after message cursing them out. Nobody calls her back.

When her calorie card is usable again, she is finally able to eat. She buys as many carrots and celery as she can get and focuses on eating that. These vegetables have so few calories that she can eat them by the pound. Even though she isn't consuming many calories, it feels like she's eating a lot. It's the only way she can get by, but knows it won't work for long. She's tried it many times in the past.

While at the hotel, Tori gets several texts from her exercise bike:

> DARREN II: Time to exercise!
>
> DARREN II: Are *you* ready to get *fit* with U-Fit?
>
> DARREN II: It's never too late to get fit with U-Fit!
>
> DARREN II: Want extra calories so that you can afford that delicious dessert you've been eying all week? Earn them with your U-Fit exercise bike!
>
> DARREN II: Don't be a Fatty Patty. Exercise every day so that you can be a Sexy Sally!
>
> DARREN II: You need to put in the extra effort if you ever want that body you've been dreaming of.
>
> DARREN II: It's *U-Fit*, not *U-Fat*. But you're going to *get* fat unless you *use* U-Fit!

The messages only get worse and worse, and Tori groans louder with each one she reads. Whoever writes these automated messages must be the most annoying person on the planet.

But then the messages begin to get more personal.

> DARREN II: You've had a few good workout sessions so far, but all that will go to waste if you take too much time off.
>
> DARREN II: Are you going to exercise again soon? It's been so long. I'm worried about you.

Tori wonders if these are automated messages at all. It sounds like somebody's actually writing them just for her.

> DARREN II: You really should exercise more. You'll regret it if you don't.
>
> DARREN II: You signed a contract. Why aren't you exercising?
>
> DARREN II: This isn't funny any more, Tori.

She realizes she was right. These aren't automated texts. They are written specifically for her. Not only that, but they must be coming from the exercise bike itself. She has no idea how the thing can write texts. She wonders if its brain is somehow linked into the U-Fit computer system. Maybe it can send texts telepathically.

Now that she knows where they are coming from, the messages begin to make her skin crawl.

> DARREN II: Where the fuck are you?
>
> DARREN II: Do you know how much money I invested in this? You *owe* me.
>
> DARREN II: You are seriously beginning to piss me off.
>
> DARREN II: GET THE FUCK OVER HERE AND RIDE ME YOU FUCKING BITCH!!!

Tori throws her phone across the room. The messages keep coming in. One every two minutes for the next three hours. But she refuses to read them. She won't even touch her phone to turn it off.

# CHAPTER NINE

Tori realizes she has to go home eventually. She doesn't know if the U-Fit people responsible for The Darren II received any of her messages. If they didn't, then nobody has done anything about the bike, nobody has even been feeding it. She likes the idea of starving the bike. It's payback for taking all of her calories away. But she doesn't want to kill it. The thing deserves worse than death, but she doesn't want to go to jail for neglecting it.

Though a part of her wonders if she actually would go to jail if it died. If all of this came to the attention of the public during a trial, Tori doubts the U-Fit company would come out of it unscathed. It would be a PR disaster. And if she tells people about how she was sexually assaulted by their equipment, she might even come out on top. It might be *them* who are the ones who face jail time.

She decides it might be time to get a lawyer. All she has to do is go home and get the contract, collect any evidence of the existence of The Darren II—such as the instruction manual, pictures of the bike, maybe even a bucket of Bike Food—and bring it to a lawyer.

If she can get somebody to believe her, somebody who will fight for her, she'll probably be able to rid herself of this nightmare.

As she's about to leave the hotel room, there is a knock at the door. It's too early to be housekeeping. When she looks through the peephole, she sees a group of men in black suits. They look like they're from the FBI.

When Tori opens the door, they stare at her with calm expressions.

"Victoria Manetti?" one of them asks.

Tori nods. "Yes, is there a problem?"

The man pulls out a badge. "We're from U-Fit Security. We'd like to have a few words with you."

The badge is similar to a police badge but with the U-Fit logo in the center. By the serious expressions on their faces, these men seem to take their job far too seriously. They seem more like mafia hitmen than U-Fit employees. Tori looks them up and down, wondering why they're here or how they tracked her down.

"What do you want?" Tori asks, raising the tone of her voice. "Is this about the messages I sent? I didn't think anybody got them. Somebody needs to do something about that thing."

They just stare at her. She's not sure if they have any idea of what she's talking about. "We have some things that need to be discussed. Confidentially. May we come in?"

Tori shrugs and backs away to let them in. Two men enter the room and close the door. The third man waits outside. She wasn't expecting guests, so the place is a mess. Food wrappers are piled on tables and by the television. The bedding is in a large ball on the bed. Wet towels are all over the floor. But the men in black suits don't seem to notice the condition of the room.

"Have a seat," says the man in black, pointing at the bed.

The other man doesn't say anything. He just stands with his back to the door, as though guarding it so that Tori doesn't try to escape.

"I'll stand," Tori says.

The man repeats himself, "Sit."

These men are beginning to worry her. They don't seem like they're here to help her or even question her. They seem like they're here to cut her throat and make it look like an accident. She did threaten to sue the U-Fit company. She was planning on getting a lawyer and exposing them for what they did to her. These men could possibly be damage control, there to get rid of her before she becomes a problem.

Tori sits on the bed. The man in black just stares at her for a few minutes, intentionally trying to intimidate her.

"Why are you in this hotel?" he asks.

Tori is thrown off by the question. "I don't know. I was…"

The man cuts her off. "Why aren't you at home riding your exercise bike?"

"Because it's disgusting. I'm never riding that thing again."

"But you signed a contract."

"The contract was misleading. Nobody ever said the

bike would try to fuck me while I rode it."

"The contract was very specific. You ride and maintain the exercise bike for a full year. You are not permitted to go on vacation during this time. You should not be staying at hotels or leaving the bike alone for longer than a twenty-four hour period. It is all in the paperwork you signed."

Tori shakes her head. "I don't remember anything like that. Besides, I don't care what the contract says. I won't do it anymore."

The man in black lets out a sigh and leans against the dresser. "That's where you're wrong. You *will* continue. In fact, the contract has been upgraded. You will now be required to ride The Darren II for at least one hour per day. You will not harm it. You will not insult it, no matter how disturbed you are by its functions. And your contract will go for as long as The Darren II wishes. *It* will decide when you can stop using it. You don't have a choice in the matter."

Tori doesn't care who might be listening through the walls. She yells at him in her loudest voice, "You can't force me to do that. Fuck you." Tori stands up. "Here's how it's going to go: you're going to go to my apartment, pick up that thing, and then get the fuck out of my life for good. If I ever see it in my house again I'm going to beat it to death with a hammer."

The man nods. "I think it's in your best interest to reconsider."

"There's nothing you can do to make me reconsider. I want that thing gone."

The man in black turns to his partner and says, "Bring him in."

His partner opens the door and signals to the man outside. A few minutes later, a familiar face is brought into the hotel room. Tori goes silent. She falls back onto the bed and inches away from them as Federico enters the room.

"It's good to see you again, Miss Manetti," Federico says.

His face is bandaged up, covering the area where his nose used to be. Large swelling and bruising on his skull where she hit him with the spinner. She can't believe it. She has no idea why he's still alive.

"I thought I killed you," Tori cries.

Federico smiles. "Killed? No, no. I could never be killed by a little thing like you."

"Well, you were *deformed* by a little thing like me." Then she smiles back.

Federico laughs, but only to cover up his anger. He obviously wants to murder her with his bare hands for disfiguring him the way she did.

The man in black gets between them so that it doesn't escalate. He looks at Tori, "We have heard about your issue with Mr. Ferlisi here. You're lucky we ran into him before he found you. You surely would have ended up on the menu in one of his fine restaurants."

Tori spits in Federico's direction, but the wad of saliva misses and hits the television screen behind him.

The man in black continues, "We have made a deal with him. He is not to go anywhere near you until your contract with us has expired."

Her mouth drops open. She looks at Federico. The Sicilian just smiles at her.

"Are you fucking kidding me?" Tori cries.

"This isn't a joke, Miss Manetti. Your life now depends on you fulfilling your end of the contract. You will still be paid. Everything will go on as it was supposed to. You just have to ride your exercise bike."

"But why should I bother?" Tori says. "Once the contract expires, he's going to kill me anyway."

"Not necessarily," says the man in black. "If The Darren II is happy with the arrangement, he can extend the contract indefinitely. You can live a full, happy life. All you have to do is put in the extra effort to keep The Darren II satisfied."

Tori feels like a cornered animal. She wants to lash out at them. Kill them all where they stand. But she's powerless. There's nothing she can do.

Federico enjoys watching her squirm. The smug, contented smile won't leave his face as he stares Tori down. "It's okay. I'm a very patient man. I can wait for your contract to expire."

He steps close to Tori and leans into her face, almost daring her to try to bite him again. "I know Darren Oscarson. He'll tire of you eventually, just as he has with all of his other whores. Once that happens, I'll be waiting for you."

Before they escort him from the room, he turns back and says one more thing, "I'll keep my sausage grinder ready for you."

The U-Fit men give Tori a new contract to sign. She doesn't bother reading it. She just signs. There's nothing else she can do.

She wonders what Federico said about being friends with Darren Oscarson. She hasn't given much thought to Darren's life before he became an exercise bike. She assumed he was just some rich old pervert with some connection to U-Fit. Perhaps he was even their CEO at one time. But if he was friends with Federico, he must have had some connection to the criminal underworld. She also wonders about the U-Fit people. They, too, seem like they have connections. These men in her room are more like mafia soldiers than representatives of a corporation. They surely aren't selling exercise bikes when they're not harassing Tori. She wonders if the whole U-Fit company is somehow involved with everything that's going on in the junk food underground. Perhaps they even run the whole thing. She knows they played a big part in getting the health laws passed. She wonders if the whole calorie system was just a conspiracy to raise the cost of junk food and exercise equipment a hundred times over.

When she looks up at the man in black, she's tempted to pick his brain over everything he knows. But she decides it would be best if she didn't know for sure one way or the other.

"We've done some upgrades to your apartment while you've been away," says the man in black. "We've installed a larger refrigerator for bike food. Your spare room has now been transformed into a proper exercise room, up to The Darren II's standards. Your closet has been fitted with a new assortment of workout attire. If you don't want to wear any of the outfits, you are permitted to work out in the nude."

Tori shrugs, disinterested in what they're telling her. "Yeah, whatever." Then she hands back the contract.

"We've also invited a friend of Mr. Oscarson to live with you."

Tori snaps out of her funk. "What?"

"Don't worry. He won't take up much space."

"I don't want to live with some strange man."

"Well, he's not exactly a man. Not anymore. He has similar tastes as Mr. Oscarson did before his transformation."

"Are you kidding me?"

"You will of course be paid extra. Another ten thousand a month."

"Another exercise bike? I'm not riding another fucking exercise bike."

The man shakes his head. "This one isn't an exercise bike."

"Well then what the hell is he?"

The man moves toward the door. Before he leaves, he says, "You'll see."

When Tori gets home, she searches her apartment for the new freak. There's nothing upstairs. They completely reconstructed her kitchen—not sure if they got permission from the apartment manager or not—but nothing living is hiding there.

Down in the exercise room, The Darren II is standing proudly in the center of the brand new ceramic floor. Mirrors have been installed on all the walls so that he can see her while she rides him. There are weights, yoga mats, even a sound system for playing music while exercising. It's still small, but it looks professional, like a real fitness center. But The Darren II is the only piece of exercise equipment she sees. There aren't any other human machines in here as the man in black said there would be.

After searching the rest of her apartment, even her bedroom and balcony, she still can't find any sign of it. Not until she has to go to the bathroom.

Without paying attention, reading a fashion magazine, she pulls down her pants and sits on the toilet. Her butt cheeks press against something warm and fleshy that shudders eagerly beneath her.

She screams and jumps away, falling to the floor with her pants around her ankles. When she looks back, she sees it on her bathroom floor, installed into the house's plumbing.

"No…" she cries. "You can't be serious…"

It is a human toilet. The thing is even more disgusting than the exercise bike, even less human. None of it is made of porcelain. The whole toilet is human flesh. The man's arms and legs have been removed. Its mouth has been stretched out to the size of a toilet bowl. Its lips have been fitted with enormous toilet seat-shaped implants. Its anus is bonded to the floor.

Tori stands and pulls her pants up. Tiny human eyes stare up at her from the inside of the toilet bowl. She can't believe they did this. She has no idea how it's even possible. But somehow they turned a man into a real human toilet. The shape and size is exact. The bowl is filled with a saliva-like fluid. The hole at the bottom was once a man's throat. Its entire digestive system is somehow connected to the plumbing.

She pulls a handle-shaped chunk of flesh and the toilet flushes. The human eyes close tight as it refills with water.

"Bizarre…" Tori says.

She doesn't know what else to say about it.

No longer having to go to the bathroom, she turns off the light and leaves it in darkness. That thing is going to be even more difficult to live with than The Darren II. She really wishes she would have taken the larger apartment when she moved in, the one with two baths. It's not going to be easy shitting in the thing's mouth every time she has to go to the bathroom.

For days, Tori disappears into her own world. She rides the human exercise bike. She shits in the human toilet. But she doesn't feel anything. Not even disgust. She becomes like a walking zombie, like she's dead inside.

The scumbags beat her. There's nothing she can do but accept her fate. Even the extra calories mean nothing to her. Food is just fuel. Her hunger is finally satisfied, but the act of eating is no longer enjoyable. The only time she eats wasps is when they escape from the taped hole in the wall.

She doesn't go to work anymore. She didn't even bother telling her boss she quit. With all the money she makes, she won't likely have to ever work again. All she does is mope around her house, eating, sleeping, shitting, and exercising. She watches television, reads articles on the internet, cleans her house and inhuman house guests, and just exists.

Melanie, her apartment manager, still bugs her to use her exercise bike on a regular basis. Tori decides to go ahead and let her see it, just to get her off her back. The look of horror on the annoying bitch's face when she walks into her exercise room is almost enough to make Tori laugh for the first time in weeks. Melanie doesn't come near her apartment anymore.

Just when Tori thinks her life couldn't get any worse, she takes a pregnancy test and gets a positive result. She's pregnant with the exercise bike's child. It took a long time for her to notice the signs, too depressed to think the morning sickness was anything but a psychological reaction to her new lifestyle. By the time she realized what might be the cause, it was too late to abort. She's going to be a mother.

Sometimes Tori ponders how her situation has come about. She doesn't understand why a man like Darren

Oscarson would force this life upon her. Not because he's a sick fetishist who wants to live out his fantasy of becoming a human exercise bike, but because he has given her no other choice. If he's a man who wishes to be dominated by a woman, who wants to be treated as something less than human, why would he force this upon her against her will? He's the one with all the power. He's the one who has control over what she does and when she does it, upon penalty of death. She doesn't know how this lifestyle would be satisfying to a man like him.

In the end, it's like she's the exercise bike and he's the one riding her.

# CHAPTER TEN

Tori comes home one night to find Federico sitting in her living room. He has a glass of wine in his hand. He's visibly drunk.

He doesn't say anything at first, just sipping his wine, reclining on her couch like he's just had the roughest day of his life. Tori puts her groceries on the floor and goes to him. She takes the bottle of wine from the coffee table and swigs a third of the bottle.

She sees that his nose has healed nicely. It's just a gaping red hole on his face that he doesn't bother covering up. The sight of it makes her smile, at least for a second.

When he notices she's staring at his deformity, Federico finally speaks.

"Pretty, aren't I?" he asks, speaking in a calm, deep tone.

Tori takes another sip and then responds, "Prettier than you were before I bit your nose off."

He nods. "My wife and kids would strongly disagree with you."

Tori sits in the chair across from him. "I didn't think

you were married."

"I guess I'm not anymore. My wife just left me."

"Because of your nose?"

"You could say that."

He pauses to pull a large caliber pistol from his coat and rests it on his lap.

Then he continues, "I made a huge mistake letting you live. Oscarson's people might have paid me a hefty sum to stay away from you, but that was nothing compared to what I lost."

"It's just a nose," Tori says. "Big fucking deal."

"I'm not talking about the nose. I could live without that. What you took from me is far more than just my charming good looks."

He finishes his glass of wine and points the revolver at her.

"I lost respect," he says. "A skinny whore like you bites off my nose and I just let you walk. Do you know how that made me look? My business isn't like it used to be. Far more money in it than before. Much bigger sharks to compete with. And the only way to survive is to be the biggest shark in the water."

"So they think you're weak now?" Tori says, cracking a smile. The gun pointed at her face doesn't intimidate her in the slightest.

"They think I'm nothing. I'm getting pushed out, tossed aside. I'll probably be dead by the end of the week."

Tori just laughs in his face.

Federico's tone goes from calm to livid. "What's so funny?"

"You said you could never be killed by a little thing like me," Tori says. "But it looks like I've killed you after all."

The man sneers and waves her words away with his gun. "You didn't kill me. I did this. I never should have taken the deal. It's my fault I chose the money over your life."

"So you're here to kill me?" Tori asks. "You're trying to fix your mistake?"

"Oh, I'm here to kill you. But it won't fix my mistake. I just want to see you die."

Tori stands up. "Then what are you waiting for? You'd be doing me a favor."

"No, it won't be so easy. I'm going to make sure you suffer."

"I'm already suffering."

She brings the bottle of wine to her lips and chugs the hearty red alcohol, waiting for him to fire. But he doesn't shoot her. He just stares, thinking of what he can do to her that will make her whimper and beg. He grinds his teeth, imagining his fingers digging through her eyes into her brain, imagining putting her through a meat grinder while she's still alive.

When Tori finishes the wine, she throws the empty bottle at his head. It hits him square in the nose, but doesn't break. As he cries at the pain, Tori goes for the gun.

"Ugly prick!" she yells in his face, struggling to pry the weapon from his fingers.

But the man is much larger than her. He grabs her by the throat and picks her off the ground, jamming the gun into her forehead.

"You fucking bitch…" he says, his wine breath hot against her eyes.

Federico drops the gun and puts his other hand around her throat, crushing her voicebox with his fingers.

"You're nothing," he says. "You're just a filthy whore."

Tori claws at his hands and face, but doesn't have the strength to break his grasp. Her vision gets blurry. The bones in her neck feel like they're crumpling, tearing apart the tender wet flesh of her esophagus.

As her arms go limp, the man throws her with all his strength. She crashes into her television set and breaks open a large hole in the wall. Thousands of wasps pour out.

"Now you die," Federico cries.

Perhaps it's because he's drunk on wine and anger. Or perhaps it's because they are so out of place, so impossible to actually be real. But the wasps don't register in his mind as he steps directly into the swarm. Not until they sting his face.

Like a storm of buzzing ferociousness, the swarm swallows them both, stinging every inch of their bodies. Federico panics, thrashing his arms around, smacking at the tiny angry insects. But Tori is used to being stung. She can take it. She crawls across the floor toward the weapon.

The Sicilian sees her going for it and tries kicking at her. But his foot only connects once before a wasp curls beneath his eyelid and stings his cornea. He screams and staggers away, trying to get to the door half-blind.

Tori shoots him in the back. He falls to his knees,

but keeps moving. She gets to her feet and walks right up to him. She presses the barrel to the back of his head.

Holding it there for a moment, allowing the wasps to sting her cheeks and nose. She snickers. It's a powerful feeling, having control of life or death over this disgusting man. She is overwhelmed with the desire to crush him, to curl him up in a tiny ball and put him in her mouth like she would a wasp or a spider, then chew him up alive.

"A little thing like me..." she tells him.

Then she blows his brains out the front of his face.

When the wasps calm down, Tori cuts up Federico's body with a dull saw and then feeds him to her human toilet one piece at a time. The eyes in the toilet glare up at her in horror as she forces the bloody chunks of man into it.

She isn't worried about getting into trouble for killing the Sicilian. If she wanted she could have just called the U-Fit people and they probably would have had somebody come over to dispose of the body for her. But that would have been weak. She's through with dealing with those people. They don't have any power over her anymore.

Once only Federico's head is left, she takes it into her exercise room and smacks The Darren II until it wakes up.

"This a friend of yours?" she asks the bike, holding the head by the scalp.

Though it can't really communicate, the bike begs for mercy. It curls in fear.

"You see this?" Her is voice deep and raspy from being choked. "This is going to be you if you piss me off."

The bike won't take its eyes off of the head. Tori isn't sure how close they were, but Darren must have known Federico enough to be disturbed by his death.

"You don't have any power over me anymore," Tori says. "You're no longer in control."

She tosses the head on the floor and then gets onto the bike. Gripping the handles tight enough to make it cringe in pain, she watches herself in the mirror, looking it in the eyes.

"Here's how things are going to go from now on," she says in a firm tone. "You are my exercise bike. That's all you are. I will no longer acknowledge you as a living being. You will not send me texts. You will not make any demands."

She puts her feet on its pedals. "You do not control my exercise schedule. I will ride you only when *I* feel like it. And when I do, I will dress in whatever I want to wear. You are nothing but a machine now. I own you."

Tori pedals the bike, riding it slowly at first, then speeding up.

"We no longer have a contract. *I* decide how long you'll be my property. And when I'm done with you, I will not send you back to your people. I will throw you in the garbage as I would any machine I've grown tired with."

She pedals the bike faster, harder. She puts so more force into it than her bike can handle. It cringes, whimpers in agony. But just before its legs break beneath Tori's feet, she steps off.

The bike pants and shivers. Sweat leaks down its frame. It stares at Tori in the mirror, admiring her strength and dominating posture as she stands over it. Her presence arouses it, causing its penis to grow hard.

When Tori sees the erection, she grabs the bike's dick. She squeezes it in her hand so tightly that the bike lets out a high-pitched squeal.

"And if you ever cum on me again, I'm going to cut this thing off and flush it down the toilet."

# CHAPTER ELEVEN

Tori becomes a new woman. She no longer sees the bike as anything but exercise equipment from that day on. It might as well be made of metal and plastic. She wouldn't even notice if it died. As long as she could still earn calories with it, she wouldn't care.

She still rides it every day, but only because she wants to earn extra calories, not giving a damn whether or not the act pleasures her machine. Sometimes she rides wearing one of the spandex outfits U-Fit provided for her, when she's in the mood, but she usually just wears smelly old sweatpants and a faded T-shirt full of holes.

The bike never complains to U-Fit about Tori's behavior. It wouldn't be able to even if it wanted to anyway, not since Tori disconnected the computer attached to its brain. Because it is supposed to just be an ordinary bike, she didn't think it necessary to allow it to communicate with the outside world. No more texting. No more communication with U-Fit or whoever else it was able to send messages to.

Tori assumes the bike must be satisfied with the

arrangement. This is what it wanted after all, isn't it? To become an inhuman machine? A machine doesn't complain. It sits there and waits to be used. That is all it's good for. Tori is giving The Darren II exactly what it wanted whether it's satisfied with the arrangement or not.

After she gets used to living this way, Tori doesn't stop with just the exercise bike and the human toilet. There are more people out there just like Darren Oscarson, who desired to be transformed into machines and furniture in order to live out their deepest sexual fantasies. As long as they are able to pay, Tori accommodates them all.

She soon finds herself surrounded by human chairs and human tables. Her bed becomes a man and his wife sewn together into a human mattress. She doesn't know where they all come from or where they were all constructed, but she accepts every one of them. The only thing she won't do is treat them as anything more than what they were designed to be.

With all the extra money she makes, Tori hires a Ukrainian immigrant to come over a few times a week to care for her human objects. Having to feed them and clean up their shit is beneath her now. It reminds her that they are actually living beings and she no longer wishes to see them in that way.

If any of the furniture shits or ejaculates when they aren't supposed to, she just throws them away without giving it a second thought. She has her Ukrainian maid drive them to the dump or drop them off at the Goodwill. Either way, she still gets paid every month. The people who deliver the money to her don't bother to check on whether she's kept them alive or not.

During flu season, sickness sweeps through her household, creating an apartment-wide pandemic of coughing, sneezing and vomiting furniture. Tori doesn't stick around to deal with this. She leaves them in her maid's care and then vacations in Japan, where she can eat all the food she wants. Even Big Macs. *Real* Big Macs.

One day, once her bank account is fatter than she'll ever need it to be, she plans to abandon all of her furniture and move to Japan for good.

When Tori's child is born, she doesn't tell The Darren II that it is his. The bike might know, or suspect, but Tori will never speak to it about the matter. There is no way she would ever admit that the father of her daughter is an exercise bike.

When her daughter is old enough, she will say that her father was a man named Dave who died in a tragedy long before she was born. She didn't know much about Dave, but she did think he was a good man. Tori feels that it's important for her daughter to believe that her father was a good man.

Maybe the bike will see its daughter grow up, watching her from the corners of its eyes when she plays with her dolls in the exercise room, but Tori doubts she'll keep the bike for that long. It's beginning to rot and stink. She's thinking about replacing it with a newer model.

There's a handsome young man she's seen eating lunch at the McDonald's every now and then. He has dark hair, deep brown eyes, and the friendliest smile she's ever seen. Tori has been thinking about asking him out, taking him to an underground bar for a few drinks, and then introducing him to a special surgeon she's acquainted with.

She just knows that he'd make an incredible exercise bike.

But becoming a human chainsaw wasn't nearly as awesome as I thought it would be. You spend most of your time just sitting in a shed.

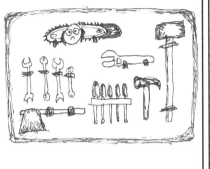

And when you're actually used, it's usually just for something stupid like cutting firewood. Which isn't only boring but you end up with tons of woodchips stuck in your teeth.

Now if there was a zombie apocalypse, being a human chainsaw would be an entirely different story. You'd be chopping heads off of zombies left and right.

And if you ever get infected with zombie blood you'd be transformed into a zombie chainsaw, which is even more awesome.

## ABOUT THE AUTHOR

**Carlton Mellick III** is one of the leading authors of the bizarro fiction subgenre. Since 2001, his books have drawn an international cult following, despite the fact that they have been shunned by most libraries and chain bookstores.

He won the Wonderland Book Award for his novel, *Warrior Wolf Women of the Wasteland*, in 2009. His short fiction has appeared in *Vice Magazine, The Year's Best Fantasy and Horror #16, The Magazine of Bizarro Fiction,* and *Zombies: Encounters with the Hungry Dead*, among others. He is also a graduate of Clarion West, where he studied under the likes of Chuck Palahniuk, Connie Willis, and Cory Doctorow.

He lives in Portland, OR, the bizarro fiction mecca.

Visit him online at **www.carltonmellick.com**

# ALSO FROM CARLTON MELLICK III AND
# ERASERHEAD PRESS
## www.eraserheadpress.com

### QUICKSAND HOUSE

Tick and Polly have never met their parents before. They live in the same house with them, they dream about them every night, they share the same flesh and blood, yet for some reason their parents have never found the time to visit them even once since they were born. Living in a dark corner of their parents' vast crumbling mansion, the children long for the day when they will finally be held in their mother's loving arms for the first time... But that day seems to never come. They worry their parents have long since forgotten about them.

When the machines that provide them with food and water stop functioning, the children are forced to venture out of the nursery to find their parents on their own. But the rest of the house is much larger and stranger than they ever could have imagined. The maze-like hallways are dark and seem to go on forever, deranged creatures lurk in every shadow, and the bodies of long-dead children litter the abandoned storerooms. Every minute out of the nursery is a constant battle for survival. And the deeper into the house they go, the more they must unravel the mysteries surrounding their past and the world they've grown up in, if they ever hope to meet the parents they've always longed to see.

Like a survival horror rendition of *Flowers in the Attic*, Carlton Mellick III's *Quicksand House* is his most gripping and sincere work to date.

### HUNGRY BUG

In a world where magic exists, spell-casting has become a serious addiction. It ruins lives, tears families apart, and eats away at the fabric of society. Those who cast too much are taken from our world, never to be heard from again. They are sent to a realm known as Hell's Bottom—a sorcerer ghetto where everyday life is a harsh struggle for survival. Porcelain dolls crawl through the alleys like rats, arcane scientists abduct people from the streets to use in their ungodly experiments, and everyone lives in fear of the aristocratic race of spider people who prey on citizens like vampires.

Told in a series of interconnected stories reminiscent of Frank Miller's *Sin City* and David Lapham's *Stray Bullets*, Carlton Mellick III's *Hungry Bug* is an urban fairy tale that focuses on the real life problems that arise within a fantastic world of magic.

## SWEET STORY

Sally is an odd little girl. It's not because she dresses as if she's from the Edwardian era or spends most of her time playing with creepy talking dolls. It's because she chases rainbows as if they were butterflies. She believes that if she finds the end of the rainbow then magical things will happen to her--leprechauns will shower her with gold and fairies will grant her every wish. But when she actually does find the end of a rainbow one day, and is given the opportunity to wish for whatever she wants, Sally asks for something that she believes will bring joy to children all over the world. She wishes that it would rain candy forever. She had no idea that her innocent wish would lead to the extinction of all life on earth.

## TUMOR FRUIT

Eight desperate castaways find themselves stranded on a mysterious deserted island. They are surrounded by poisonous blue plants and an ocean made of acid. Ravenous creatures lurk in the toxic jungle. The ghostly sound of crying babies can be heard on the wind.

Once they realize the rescue ships aren't coming, the eight castaways must band together in order to survive in this inhospitable environment. But survival might not be possible. The air they breathe is lethal, there is no shelter from the elements, and the only food they have to consume is the colorful squid-shaped tumors that grow from a mentally disturbed woman's body.

## AS SHE STABBED ME GENTLY IN THE FACE

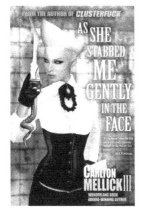

Oksana Maslovskiy is an award-winning artist, an internationally adored fashion model, and one of the most infamous serial killers this country has ever known. She enjoys murdering pretty young men with a nine-inch blade, cutting them open and admiring their delicate insides. It's the only way she knows how to be intimate with another human being. But one day she meets a victim who cannot be killed. His name is Gabriel—a mysterious immortal being with a deep desire to save Oksana's soul. He makes her a deal: if she promises to never kill another person again, he'll become her eternal murder victim.

What at first seems like the perfect relationship for Oksana quickly devolves into a living nightmare when she discovers that Gabriel enjoys being killed by her just a little too much. He turns out to be obsessive, possessive, and paranoid that she might be murdering other men behind his back. And because he is unkillable, it's not going to be easy for Oksana to get rid of him.

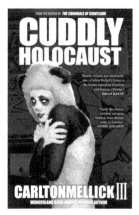

## CUDDLY HOLOCAUST

Teddy bears, dollies, and little green soldiers—they've all had enough of you. They're sick of being treated like playthings for spoiled little brats. They have no rights, no property, no hope for a future of any kind. You've left them with no other option-in order to be free, they must exterminate the human race.

Julie is a human girl undergoing reconstructive surgery in order to become a stuffed animal. Her plan: to infiltrate enemy lines in order to save her family from the toy death camps. But when an army of plushy soldiers invade the underground bunker where she has taken refuge, Julie will be forced to move forward with her plan despite her transformation being not entirely complete.

## ARMADILLO FISTS

A weird-as-hell gangster story set in a world where people drive giant mechanical dinosaurs instead of cars.

Her name is Psycho June Howard, aka Armadillo Fists, a woman who replaced both of her hands with living armadillos. She was once the most bloodthirsty fighter in the world of illegal underground boxing. But now she is on the run from a group of psychotic gangsters who believe she's responsible for the death of their boss. With the help of a stegosaurus driver named Mr. Fast Awesome—who thinks he is God's gift to women even though he doesn't have any arms or legs--June must do whatever it takes to escape her pursuers, even if she has to kill each and every one of them in the process.

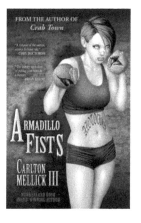

## VILLAGE OF THE MERMAIDS

Mermaids are protected by the government under the Endangered Species Act, which means you aren't able to kill them even in self-defense. This is especially problematic if you happen to live in the isolated fishing village of Siren Cove, where there exists a healthy population of mermaids in the surrounding waters that view you as the main source of protein in their diet.

The only thing keeping these ravenous sea women at bay is the equally-dangerous supply of human livestock known as Food People. Normally, these "feeder humans" are enough to keep the mermaid population happy and well-fed. But in Siren Cove, the mermaids are avoiding the human livestock and have returned to hunting the frightened local fishermen. It is up to Doctor Black, an eccentric representative of the Food People Corporation, to investigate the matter and hopefully find a way to correct the mermaids' new eating patterns before the remaining villagers end up as fish food. But the more he digs, the more he discovers there are far stranger and more dangerous things than mermaids hidden in this ancient village by the sea.

## I KNOCKED UP SATAN'S DAUGHTER

Jonathan Vandervoo lives a carefree life in a house made of legos, spending his days building lego sculptures and his nights getting drunk with his only friend—an alcoholic sumo wrestler named Shoji. It's a pleasant life with no responsibility, until the day he meets Lici. She's a soul-sucking demon from hell with red skin, glowing eyes, a forked tongue, and pointy red devil horns... and she claims to be nine months pregnant with Jonathan's baby.

Now Jonathan must do the right thing and marry the succubus or else her demonic family is going to rip his heart out through his ribcage and force him to endure the worst torture hell has to offer for the rest of eternity. But can Jonathan really love a fire-breathing, frog-eating, cold-blooded demoness? Or would eternal damnation be preferable? Either way, the big day is approaching. And once Jonathan's conservative Christian family learns their son is about to marry a spawn of Satan, it's going to be all-out war between demons and humans, with Jonathan and his hell-born bride caught in the middle.

## KILL BALL

In a city where everyone lives inside of plastic bubbles, there is no such thing as intimacy. A husband can no longer kiss his wife. A mother can no longer hug her children. To do this would mean instant disease. Ever since the disease swept across the globe, we have become isolated within our own personal plastic prison cells, rolling aimlessly through rubber streets in what are essentially man-sized hamster balls.

Colin Hinchcliff longs for the touch of another human being. He can't handle the loneliness, the confinement, and he's horribly claustrophobic. The only thing keeping him going is his unrequited love for an exotic dancer named Siren, a woman who has never seen his face, doesn't even know his name. But when The Kill Ball, a serial slasher in a black leather sphere, begins targeting women at Siren's club, Colin decides he has to do whatever it takes in order to protect her... even if he has to break out of his bubble and risk everything to do it.

## THE TICK PEOPLE

They call it Gloom Town, but that isn't its real name. It is a sad city, the saddest of cities, a place so utterly depressing that even their ales are brewed with the most sorrow-filled tears. They built it on the back of a colossal mountain-sized animal, where its woeful citizens live like human fleas within the hairy, pulsing landscape. And those tasked with keeping the city in a state of constant melancholy are the Stressmen-a team of professional sadness-makers who are perpetually striving to invent new ways of causing absolute misery.

But for the Stressman known as Fernando Mendez, creating grief hasn't been so easy as of late. His ideas aren't effective anymore. His treatments are more likely to induce happiness than sadness. And if he wants to get back in the game, he's going to have to relearn the true meaning of despair.

## THE HAUNTED VAGINA

It's difficult to love a woman whose vagina is a gateway to the world of the dead...

Steve is madly in love with his eccentric girlfriend, Stacy. Unfortunately, their sex life has been suffering as of late, because Steve is worried about the odd noises that have been coming from Stacy's pubic region. He says that her vagina is haunted. She doesn't think it's that big of a deal. Steve, on the other hand, completely disagrees.

When a living corpse climbs out of her during an awkward night of sex, Stacy learns that her vagina is actually a doorway to another world. She persuades Steve to climb inside of her to explore this strange new place. But once inside, Steve finds it difficult to return... especially once he meets an oddly attractive woman named Fig, who lives within the lonely haunted world between Stacy's legs.

## THE CANNIBALS OF CANDYLAND

There exists a race of cannibals who are made out of candy. They live in an underground world filled with lollipop forests and gumdrop goblins. During the day, while you are away at work, they come above ground and prowl our streets for food. Their prey: your children. They lure young boys and girls to them with their sweet scent and bright colorful candy coating, then rip them apart with razor sharp teeth and claws.

When he was a child, Franklin Pierce witnessed the death of his siblings at the hands of a candy woman with pink cotton candy hair. Since that day, the candy people have become his obsession. He has spent his entire life trying to prove that they exist. And after discovering the entrance to the underground world of the candy people, Franklin finds himself venturing into their sugary domain. His mission: capture one of them and bring it back, dead or alive.

## THE EGG MAN

It is a survival of the fittest world where humans reproduce like insects, children are the property of corporations, and having a ten-foot tall brain is a grotesque sexual fetish.

Lincoln has just been released into the world by the Georges Organization, a corporation that raises creative types. A Smell, he has little prospect of succeeding as a visual artist. But after he moves into the Henry Building, he meets Luci, the weird and grimy girl who lives across the hall. She is a Sight. She is also the most disgusting woman Lincoln has ever met. Little does he know, she will soon become his muse.

Now Luci's boyfriend is threatening to kill Lincoln, two rival corporations are preparing for war, and Luci is dragging him along to discover the truth about the mysterious egg man who lives next door. Only the strongest will survive in this tale of individuality, love, and mutilation.

## APESHIT

Apeshit is Mellick's love letter to the great and terrible B-horror movie genre. Six trendy teenagers (three cheerleaders and three football players) go to an isolated cabin in the mountains for a weekend of drinking, partying, and crazy sex, only to find themselves in the middle of a life and death struggle against a horribly mutated psychotic freak that just won't stay dead. Mellick parodies this horror cliché and twists it into something deeper and stranger. It is the literary equivalent of a grindhouse film. It is a splatter punk's wet dream. It is perhaps one of the most fucked up books ever written.

If you are a fan of Takashi Miike, Evil Dead, early Peter Jackson, or Eurotrash horror, then you must read this book.

## CLUSTERFUCK

A bunch of douchebag frat boys get trapped in a cave with subterranean cannibal mutants and try to survive not by using their wits but by following the bro code...

From master of bizarro fiction Carlton Mellick III, author of the international cult hits Satan Burger and Adolf in Wonderland, comes a violent and hilarious B movie in book form. Set in the same woods as Mellick's splatterpunk satire Apeshit, Clusterfuck follows Trent Chesterton, alpha bro, who has come up with what he thinks is a flawless plan to get laid. He invites three hot chicks and his three best bros on a weekend of extreme cave diving in a remote area known as Turtle Mountain, hoping to impress the ladies with his expert caving skills.

But things don't quite go as Trent planned. For starters, only one of the three chicks turns out to be remotely hot and she has no interest in him for some inexplicable reason. Then he ends up looking like a total dumbass when everyone learns he's never actually gone caving in his entire life. And to top it all off, he's the one to get blamed once they find themselves lost and trapped deep underground with no way to turn back and no possible chance of rescue. What's a bro to do? Sure he could win some points if he actually tried to save the ladies from the family of unkillable subterranean cannibal mutants hunting them for their flesh, but fuck that. No slam piece is worth that amount of effort. He'd much rather just use them as bait so that he can save himself.

## THE BABY JESUS BUTT PLUG

Step into a dark and absurd world where human beings are slaves to corporations, people are photocopied instead of born, and the baby jesus is a very popular anal probe.

www.ingramcontent.com/pod-product-compliance
Ingram Content Group UK Ltd
Pitfield, Milton Keynes, MK11 3LW, UK
UKHW040644060325
4877UKWH00015B/90